BODY
SCISSORS

BODY
SCISSORS

Jerome
Doolittle

POCKET BOOKS

New York   London   Toronto   Sydney   Tokyo   Singapore

This book is a work of fiction. Names, characters, places and
incidents are either the product of the author's imagination or
are used fictitiously. Any resemblance to actual events or
locales or persons, living or dead, is entirely coincidental.

POCKET BOOKS, a division of Simon & Schuster Inc.
1230 Avenue of the Americas, New York, NY 10020

Doolittle, Jerome.
    Body scissors : a Tom Bethany mystery / Jerome Doolittle.
        p.   cm.
    ISBN 0-671-70752-3 : $17.95
    I. Title.
PS3554.O584B58   1990
813'.54—dc20   90-38013
                                                CIP

First Pocket Books hardcover printing November 1990

10 9 8 7 6 5 4 3 2 1

Printed in the U.S.A.

To D.

BODY
SCISSORS

1

ON A PARCEL OF LAND ALONG MASSACHUSETTS AVEnue between Dunster and Holyoke streets in Cambridge, just across from Harvard Yard, is an office building called Holyoke Center. It is a ten-story concrete block that gives the appearance of having been built on the cheap, in some marginal commercial block of a city like Bangkok or Rabat. Harvard owns the ugly building. Harvard owns most of the real estate in sight. Harvard is the largest landowner in Cambridge.

One of the ground-floor tenants of Holyoke Center is a sort of bakery-café called Au Bon Pain, which pays for the use of a large, tree-shaded terrace out front. To sit there, you're supposed to be nursing a croissant or whatever. But other identical, cast-iron tables and chairs stand on the brick-cobbled plaza next to the terrace, along with three concrete tables with inlaid chess boards. And all these are for public use.

I was using one of the cast-iron tables one Friday morning in August, cool and breezy for a change, when a man stopped on the sidewalk and spotted me after a while. It was Arthur Kleber. I hadn't seen Arthur since the 1982 Democratic miniconvention in Philadelphia, where I was guarding the body of a would-be president who was then—and still was—a long way from rating Secret Service protection. Since back then in 1982, I hadn't missed Arthur Kleber even one time. And yet here he was, taking the free chair at my table just as if I had invited him to.

"Most guys, you don't have to track them down on the streets like a bag lady," he said. "Most guys got phones."

"I got a phone, too."

"Information doesn't know about it."

"It's unlisted."

"Information doesn't say, 'Sorry, sir, that party has an unlisted number.' Information never heard of you."

"It's unlisted under another name, Arthur."

"So what's the number?"

"Think about why I would have an unlisted phone under another name. Could it maybe be because I don't want people to call me? What do you think?"

"What the hell use is a phone, then?"

"It calls out okay."

"Jesus, Bethany . . ."

"Shut up a minute, Arthur, okay? Maybe we got a fight going here."

Kleber looked where I was, out at the architecturally advanced public space that Harvard Square had become since they rebuilt the old T-stop. Now there were stone benches and swooping ramps that probably the architect hadn't envisioned any practical use for, but the skateboarders quickly had. There was a kind of overgrown conversation pit, too, this side of the subway entrance.

At the moment the conversation was between two large freaks, who were shouting and shoving each other. Both of them bore tribal disfigurements, like the tiger tattooed on George Shultz's Princeton ass. One freak had a center strip of green hair growing on his otherwise shaven head; the other was a skinhead with a half dozen or so gold rings, or gold-colored rings anyway, hanging from the ear I could see. He wore leathers; black, of course, and studded. (I myself wore a J. Press jacket of khaki gabardine, summer-weight gray flannel slacks, and cordovan loafers polished to a soft shine with Meltonian Cream. Different tribe.)

"Fuck you," hollered the one with the green Mohawk.

"Fuck you, too," shouted the skinhead. But they had stopped shoving.

"Aw, hell," I said to Kleber. "They're starting to talk things out."

"You got a nice life, Bethany," Arthur said. "This is it, huh? You just sit around all day waiting for the freaks to fight?"

"At least I don't have to wait four years for the next one."

"Hey, there's midterms, too. And referendums. And special elections. Nowadays, politics is forever."

"What are you, with Markham now?"

"Yeah. Phil wants to see you."

"Jeffers?"

Kleber nodded. I looked over at the two freaks. Their hands were down; they were talking loud, but not shouting.

"Does he want to give me any money?" I asked.

"What my understanding is, yes, he does."

"Okay," I said. "Let's go."

*   *   *

Headquarters was just off Milk Street in Boston. Everything else around was high-rent: a jewelry store, two
expense-account restaurants, a gentlemen's outfitters
with bolts of British woolens gracefully draped in the
window. In the middle of all this, strung pretty nearly
halfway along the block, a banner sagged from its supporting ropes. It read MARKHAM FOR PRESIDENT NATIONAL
CAMPAIGN HEADQUARTERS in big, sloppy, red letters,
hand-painted.

"Nice location," I said to Kleber. "Somebody go bankrupt?" He didn't have to ask what I meant. We both
knew that campaigns search out troubled real estate.

"Even better," Kleber said. "Axel, Shearman moved
to smaller offices and the lease here had four months to
run."

"Nice they moved out early, out of their nice location," I said. "People that nice, I think I'll put my money
with them, I ever get any."

Plainly Axel, Shearman was putting its own money
with Senator Dan Markham. The investment banking
firm had been indicted two months before on seventy-
two federal charges. One of their flacks had written an
op-ed piece in *The New York Times* the day before,
whining that the government prosecutors shouldn't use
the racketeering laws against financial statesmen whose
nonexistent offenses were civil, not criminal. The flack's
point seemed to be that his bosses had stolen too much
money to be racketeers.

"Hey, we're paying rent for the place," Arthur said.
"The going rate, too."

"Hey, I can fly with my arms. You believe that, Arthur?"

"Fuck you, Bethany," he said, unoffended.

The headquarters was like all campaign headquarters,
busy and inefficient. Four years ago, when I was doing
some security work for the last campaign, I came across

sixty-three thousand dollars in uncashed checks the day after we lost the election—donations that had got mislaid in somebody's desk while we were canceling TV ads for lack of money. Campaigns are a lot like real wars: disorganized messes that don't get won because anybody running things on either side is smart. They get lost because one side is even stupider than the other.

Meanwhile, they use up a lot of enthusiastic and idealistic young people, and these were what was providing the high energy level of the Markham headquarters. No one sat doing nothing. Everyone in sight was on the phone or waiting for the copier, or typing or running around with papers. Out of sight the professionals would be meeting, muddling through to the decisions that would make most of this effort useless. Boss of those professionals this time was Phil Jeffers, who had earned the job of campaign manager by being deputy campaign manager in the Democratic party's last overwhelming defeat. The man who had been campaign manager that time was now getting rich with his own consulting firm, which had Senator Markham's campaign as its principal client. Failing upward is an established route to the top in politics; take a look at Bush's résumé.

Kleber stuck his head into a door and said something I couldn't hear. After listening a moment he pulled his head back out and said, "Phil's tied up in a meeting. We'll go see Billy Fuller."

"Who's he?"

"Phil's deputy. The administrative guy."

"Let's see Markham instead."

"Come on, Bethany. The senator isn't even in town."

"Okay, so long."

"What do you mean, so long?"

"You came looking for me, Arthur, remember? Not the

other way around. Phil isn't talking to me and I'm not talking to the administrative guy, so it's so long."

"Jesus, Tom . . ." Now it was Tom.

I looked at Kleber until he stuck his head back inside the door. In a minute Phil Jeffers came out. Nearly as he let me know from his big smile and hearty handclasp, his meeting had turned out to be a terrible waste of time and he was glad to get out of it. He took me to a little room down the hall that had probably been a closet back when Axel, Shearman was floating junk bonds and swindling its clients from these offices. He gave me the only chair in the room, and himself sat on the desk. Not only was this polite, it also gave him the height advantage. People like Jeffers think things like that are important.

"The campaign needs you, Tom," he started out.

"Well, I don't need the campaign. Frankly, I don't give a damn if Tweedledum wins in November or Tweedledee does."

Jeffers smiled, as if I had said something lovable. "Same old Tom," he said. He even shook his head in mock exasperation. "Same old pain in the ass."

"You knew that when you sent Kleber to find me. So a pain in the ass has got to be what you're looking for."

"It is. Let me tell you where the senator is headed."

It turned out that Senator Markham wanted to kick off his campaign on Labor Day, four weeks away, by announcing his choice for secretary of state. I figured this would mean that every other plausible candidate for the job would immediately bail out of the campaign and start sniping from the sidelines, if he didn't go over to the other side entirely. But I probably hadn't been called in for my political advice, and so I didn't offer it.

"Of course the big risk is we could wind up dragging an Eagleton or a Ferraro behind us for the rest of the campaign," Jeffers went on. "That's where you come in."

"Why me? Use your lawyers to woodshed the guy."

"Yeah, right. The way McGovern and Mondale did. No, this time we want somebody objective, from outside. Somebody with a different kind of mentality."

"What kind of mentality?"

"An investigative mentality."

"Is that the way Markham put it?"

"What difference does it make how he put it?"

"Not a bit. Five thousand dollars a week, payable in advance each Monday in a cashier's check made out to Infotek." I spelled it for him. "Plus expenses. I'll trust you over the weekend for the expenses. I'll put in for them every Friday for the previous week and you can add them to Monday's check."

"That's ridiculous. I could hire Ellison or Futterman and his guys for a quarter of that."

"Hire them, then."

"Come on, Tom. The campaign can't afford that kind of money."

"Why not? You pay that kind of money every day to political con men that couldn't find their ass with both hands. The difference between them and me is I know what I'm doing. And you know I do, or you wouldn't be trying to hire somebody that you don't like a goddamn bit more than I like you."

"Now that right there. That's the mentality we want."

"I know. Who's your guy?"

"Kellicott."

"Does he know you want him?"

"He knows he's under consideration."

"Call him and tell him you're aiming me at him."

"All right."

"Today's Friday. If I've got the money Monday I'll go over and see him, get started."

"Where do we send the check?"

"Messenger it over to Charles at the Tasty. He works six A.M. to four."

"The fuck is the Tasty?"

"Just send your guy to Harvard Square and tell him to look around till he sees a sign says Tasty. It's a lunch counter."

We didn't shake hands when I left, which was a sign that our new professional relationship was starting out on a realistic footing. Another sign was that Jeffers hadn't even bothered to sound offended when I insisted on prepayment. We both knew that only a fool lets a preacher or a politician run a tab.

Monday at nine, an hour when honest people are at work, I was at the Tasty having breakfast. The Tasty isn't much to look at, but it's durable. The most modern thing about it is the neon sign in the window saying the place was established in 1916. The equipment and furnishings suggest that this is true. The chromed stools along the counter have worn oak tops. The pattern on the yellow countertop has been mostly rubbed off. Here and there the dark brown stuff underneath shows through the yellow.

Along the counter are five steel struts, the chrome long since pitted, that support circular platforms a little bigger than pie plates. Each has three tiers, probably meant for three pies, but now the racks hold doughnuts and various pastries. Plastic covers protect them from flies and customers. Underneath all this, on the counter itself, are glass cookie jars full of bagels and muffins. In whatever room is left, you arrange your own food the best way you can.

The Tasty is laid out on the same general lines as a

U-boat, except not quite as wide and only eleven stools long. Along the left wall are a cigarette machine, a Coke machine, a glass-covered case displaying a T-shirt that says "Tasty College" on it, and four more stools with a shelf for your food in front of them. And back there in the rear was a pay phone and a stamp machine, which fully met my office needs most of the time. The rest of the time, there was the Au Bon Pain terrace, Widener Library, the Harvard faculty club, and the various waiting rooms in the Harvard University health services, a few steps away. The Tasty, though, was the only one of these places where they knew my name.

"Is there a Charles here?" asked a kid with an ROTC crew cut. What goes around comes around. When I was his age, the hard hats were cleanshaven and short-haired. Now it's the college kids, and the truck drivers wear the beards.

"This is your lucky day," the counterman answered the kid. "I'm Charles."

"Oh, good. I've got something for a Mr. Tom Bethany."

"You still lucky, then. That's him down at the end."

The kid looked at me and nodded politely. "I'm supposed to deliver it to Charles," he said to Charles. "In your hand."

"I see your point," Charles said. "I wouldn't trust him neither." He took the kid's envelope and handed it to me.

"I'm sorry," the kid said to me. "But Mr. Jeffers specifically said Charles, in his hand." Jeffers was still terrorizing the troops, apparently.

"No problem," I said, and the kid left happy.

After breakfast I managed to cash the cashier's check from the Markham for President campaign at a branch of the bank that had issued it, with no more than the usual amount of hassle that banks give you over parting with money they owe you. Then I deposited the five thousand dollars cash in another bank, in one of the several accounts I'm always opening and closing in several names and in different places. Cash leaves no paper trail, or not much.

And then I went back to my room to dress for the meeting I had scheduled with Professor Kellicott. Phil Jeffers, a small man, tries always to occupy the high ground. Tom Bethany, a man to the polyester born, makes it a point to be at least as well-dressed as anyone he goes up against. And so I picked out a blue cord suit tailored by Southwick, twenty dollars secondhand from Keezer's and another thirty-five for slight alterations. Shirts and ties I buy new, but from Filene's basement. Dress shoes they've got you on, though. You can't cut corners on shoes. I bought mine from Lobb's of London, when I was coming back from the war in 1974, flush with money for the first time in my life. I had them make me four pairs, two black and two brown, and if they ever wear out, my lasts are on file.

On the way out I stopped to clear the occupant ads out of my mailbox, which had the name Tom Carpenter on it. The only nonadvertising mail that ever came was Tom Carpenter's phone bill, and it wasn't that time of month. Carpenter was the name my phone was unlisted under, and the name my neighbors and landlord knew me by. The best security isn't bars and alarms; it's when people who don't like you can't look up your address.

The weather had turned hot over the weekend, and I strolled down Harvard Street, in the shade wherever I could manage it. The trick to dealing with heat is to keep your movements slow and smooth, as if you were underwater. Professor Kellicott probably didn't have to worry about these things, since his station in life and his wife's money made it pretty certain that he would be air-conditioned most of the time.

I didn't start out entirely neutral about J. Alden Kellicott, Phillips Professor of Political Economy at the John F. Kennedy School of Government. For one thing, he parted his name on the left like my old high school principal, C. Darwin Feuerbach. You had to ask yourself what was wrong with Charles. Or John, in Kellicott's case, since he was presumably descended from the Mayflower's youngest Puritan. The second problem I had with the professor was that his brilliant career in academia and government had brought him to the top of America's foreign policy establishment. And for a good many years in Laos, I had been on the receiving end of America's foreign policy.

Kellicott's office wasn't air-conditioned and he was in shirt sleeves. His tie, still knotted, hung from the back of a chair. The tie blew in the wind from a floor fan as tall as a man, the kind you still see now and then in barbershops old enough to have a striped pole outside.

"Here, sit where you can catch some of the breeze," he said. "Take off your coat."

And so I took it off. I didn't want to be any worse-dressed than him, either.

"I used to have a sore throat all summer from the damned air-conditioning," he went on, taking my coat from me and hanging it on the chair by his tie. "This spring I found out that Harvard has a whole basement full of these old fans. Sorry to make you suffer for my sore throat."

"The fan's fine, Professor Kellicott."

"Call me Alden. My parents christened me Jephthah, as if I didn't have enough trouble as it was. Jesus, I was already a skinny little kid with glasses."

I nodded, but I certainly wasn't going to call him

11

Alden. I would call him nothing. "Phil Jeffers told you what I'm up to, I guess," I said.

"You're my official biographer. I'm supposed to open my soul to you."

"I'll get most of it elsewhere. For now, the main thing I'll need from you is access."

"Whatever I can do."

"I need a blanket letter on letterhead stationery, authorizing whoever it may concern to talk to me fully and frankly."

"Won't that get around? Dan doesn't want news of all this to leak before he's ready to announce it, I'm sure."

"Introduce me in the letter as a free-lance writer, working on a profile of you. With your full cooperation and support."

"All right. What else?"

"I need letters to all your old schools back to first grade. Giving them permission to release your records to me."

"Will they do that?"

"Maybe, maybe not. They certainly won't without a letter of authorization. I'll need one for your doctor or doctors, too. Psychiatrists, psychologists, or counselors, if any. And for your accountant."

Kellicott was making notes. "No problem," he said. "If you want to wait around after we're through, I'll have my girl do all this up. Well, we don't say 'girl' anymore, do we?" He was completely matter-of-fact about it all, as if strangers pawed over his life as a regular thing. No reluctance at all; not even curiosity over what I expected to find in, for example, his first-grade report cards. I expected to find nothing, actually, but my way of working is to rake together as big a pile of facts as I can. Then I look for patterns, incongruities, relationships between this thing and that. Whatever. If I knew exactly what I was looking for, I wouldn't have to look. I'd go straight to it.

"And I'd like a copy of your most recent Standard Form Eighty-six," I said. "That's the biographical form you filled out for your government security clearance. Also your financial disclosure forms from when you were in the State Department and your income tax returns as far back as you've got them."

"Between my secretary and myself, we should be able to put together everything you need."

Kellicott had a wonderful voice. It was deep and warm and it carried well. If he had read out a list of the day's ten most active stocks in that voice, you'd have thought he was saying something grave and wise. I've seen stuff about the advantages that height and good looks and slimness give to the people who happen to be born with them, but nobody seems to study the role that voices play. In my basic training company there was a kid from Illinois with a voice you could hear from one end of the barracks to the other. That voice was enough to convince the dummy noncoms to make him a platoon leader, wearing an armband with temporary sergeant stripes on it. With this head start he became a real squad leader in Vietnam, and a sniper aimed for his real stripes. So maybe that voice was enough to make him dead, too.

Kellicott's voice would probably have made him a general, just as William Westmoreland's looks had made him one. But all Westmoreland had was the looks, whereas Kellicott had brains along with his command voice. For looks the professor was average, a slightly gawky six-foot ectomorph with a pleasant, homely face.

"You know about my daughter, don't you?" he asked—a statement more than a question.

"Not much. I read the papers at the time. If they ever caught the guy, I missed it."

"They never caught him. It seems to me they should have, but the Cambridge police aren't the FBI."

"Why should they have caught him?"

"It wasn't in the papers, but there were initials on her."

"On her?"

"Carved." His voice wavered a little on the word, and he stopped talking till he could get a hold of himself. "It doesn't matter," he went on, still with a hint of unsteadiness. "We don't really want to know who did it, anymore. We've tried to move on. You have to."

Kellicott got up and looked out the window, his back to me, for a long moment. Then his posture straightened slightly, and he turned away and sat back down.

"I'm sorry," he said. "I think I can talk about it after all this time, and mostly I can. But sometimes it comes back on me."

"I know," I said. "There are things in Southeast Asia that I thought I'd be over by now, but they come back on me, too."

Kellicott jumped at the change of subject. "Vietnam?"

"A few klicks into it sometimes, but mostly Laos."

"Were you with the military or the embassy?"

"First with the military, then sort of with the embassy."

"You don't look like someone who was sort of with the embassy. Of course, you don't look like my idea of a private detective, either. Maybe it's the glasses."

"I'm not a private detective. I'm sort of a researcher, sort of a security consultant."

Kellicott smiled. "I bet you are. Phil Jeffers says you're sort of a wrestler, too. You don't look like my idea of a wrestler, either."

"Real wrestlers don't look like anything special. Not

14

like Hulk Hogan. He may know how to wrestle, for all I know, but that isn't what he does for a living."

"Well, I hope I'm sort of a teacher the way you're sort of a wrestler. Phil says you made the Olympic team in 1980. The team that wasn't."

"Yeah, well, Carter and I wanted to send a signal to the Russians. We were pretty pissed off over Afghanistan."

"I argued as strongly as I could against it, but you see how far I got," Kellicott said. "The boycott was a totally futile gesture."

"I don't know. It just took a while to work."

"Eight years is a while, all right," Kellicott said. He shook his head, over the folly of Jimmy Carter and Olympic boycotts. "You take it well, I've got to say. I can't imagine what it must have felt like to train at that level for what? Years at least. And then have it all snatched away from you."

"You don't have to imagine. Just remember what you felt when Reagan beat Carter."

Kellicott smiled again. "I guess that's right," he said. "Of course, what the papers were saying might not have happened. I didn't know for sure that I would have been secretary of state in a second term."

"I didn't know for sure that I'd win a medal, either."

"I suppose the point is that neither of us got the chance to compete," Kellicott said. He paused for a moment, looking down almost as if he were shy. "I wonder if Dan Markham appreciates what he's got in you," he said at last.

It was unlikely that Senator Markham did; I was just a sharp instrument to be used for special jobs. I waited to see where Kellicott was going with this.

"Have you ever considered going back into the government?" he asked.

"Not really."

"The State Department's security operation has gotten a lot bigger over the past decade, but it hasn't gotten a lot better. If everything comes together, I'll be looking for somebody ..." His voice trailed off, and then he came firmly out of his reverie. "Well, let me take you out to Mrs. Weintraub so you can explain to her exactly what you need."

And so he took me out to Mrs. Weintraub, and pretty soon I was back at one of the black cast-iron tables outside Holyoke Center, thinking about running the State Department's security office for Secretary of State Kellicott. But thinking about it was as close as I would ever come, since my style of life depends on escaping bureaucratic notice at all levels, from the federal government down to Harvard University.

I took out of my briefcase the fat, three-subject spiral notebook I had just bought and began to set down my conversation with Professor Kellicott. I don't use tape recorders for routine interviews, because people talk differently when they know the recorder is going. But I can re-create even a long conversation pretty nearly word-for-word if I can get at the job soon afterward. I know, because I used to check myself against the tape, until I decided that hidden recorders were a waste of time.

When I had finished setting the conversation down, I read it through twice. I saw nothing to change the impression I had formed of Kellicott during the interview. He was good the way Peggy Lee is good: so good you have to listen hard to tell how good she is.

Then I crossed the street, entered Harvard Yard, and headed for the stacks to fill up as much as I could of my new, 150-page notebook. I started out in the reference room at Widener Library, which is pretty nearly the size of two basketball courts laid end to end. It's a public facility, and so a lot of the readers, like me, have no connection with Harvard. God knows what sad and curious notions, manias, obsessions, mad delusions they pursue all day. Which one will end up in tomorrow's Texas Book Depository? Which is Karl Marx? And who is this peculiar stray, this mesomorph with reading glasses? Why has he spent so many thousands of hours in this building over the years? At least this time I was getting paid, though. I only left, as reluctantly as the other stack rats, when they closed the joint at quarter till ten.

Next morning, Tuesday, I was there at nine when the government documents section opened. All day and Wednesday as well, I spent going through transcripts of congressional hearings and the microfilmed files of *The Washington Post*, *The New York Times*, the *Los Angeles Times*, *The Boston Globe*, and *The Wall Street Journal*. J. Alden Kellicott had left a considerable paper trail behind him during his three years as assistant secretary of state for Latin American affairs, and he had done nearly as well before and after his stint in Washington. Whenever Kellicott had a few minutes to spare, it seemed, he would knock out another op-ed piece or magazine article or contribution to a scholarly journal. Or get himself interviewed on television. Or give a speech. Or write a book.

He had written five altogether, mostly on something he called global interlock. Interlock seemed an odd word, but the books were familiar enough. What they offered was the same old insecure self-doubt, alternately bragging and whimpering, wrapped for sales purposes in red, white, and blue, that Kissinger and Brzezinski had been peddling to the suckers all along. Only those two had already laid claim to the respective brand names of global architecture and global mosaic, leaving Kellicott stuck with global interlock.

Kellicott, the public man, presented himself to the world this way:

Kellicott, J. Alden, educator, former government official; b. Sharon, Conn., March 19, 1938; m. Susan Leffingwell Milton, June 20, 1960; children: Emily, Phyllis. B.A., Yale, 1959; M.A., Harvard, 1961; lectr. government, 1961; asst. prof., 1962; Ph.D., Harvard, 1964; Inst. de Science Politique, U. of Paris, 1964–65; assoc. prof. Harvard, 1966; assoc. dir. Harvard's Center for Internat. Affairs, 1967; prof. government, Harvard, 1968; Asst. Sec. of State, Latin American affairs, 1977–80; Phillips prof. pol. econ., JFK School of Govt., 1981—. Author: Politics of Paucity: Political Stability in the Sahel, 1965; Deterring Doomsday: The Nuclear Interlock, 1968; Reconstructing Interlock: The Challenge of the Post-Carter Years, 1982; Rim of Revolution: Asia's Technological Challenge, 1984; The Non-nuclear Umbrella: Beyond Disarmament, 1987.

As Who's Who entries go, that was nicely stripped down. A man with less self-confidence wouldn't have left it at B.A., Yale, 1959, for instance. Kellicott could have added "summa cum laude, Phi Beta Kappa, Scroll and Key, winner of the Snow scholarship, and of the de Forest Prize for public speaking." He could have mentioned that his doctoral dissertation at Harvard won the Sumner Prize. He could have listed the learned societies he belonged to, the journals and magazines he had written for, his trusteeships and directorships and honorary degrees. And his clubs, the Metropolitan in Washington and the River in New York.

I found all these things out in other reference books, and in various articles I dug out of the newspaper microfilms and the Widener Library's collection of magazine back files. But there was one omission from Kellicott's *Who's Who* entry that I couldn't fill in. Between their own names and the names of their spouses, most respondents listed the names of their parents. Since the format of the entries was standard, presumably the compilers worked from a form that the subjects filled out. Kellicott must have failed to fill in that particular blank. A little break in the pattern, then, and anomalies are one of the things I look for. The closest I could come to filling in the blank was a sentence in an old *New York Times* profile of the then-new assistant secretary of state: "Professor Kellicott grew up in the little town of Sharon, Connecticut, where his father operated a local transportation firm."

The rest of the biographical stuff that I got out of the library's back files just fleshed out the entry in *Who's Who*. If Kellicott had ever faltered on his way up the university and government ladder, no evidence of it appeared. Fresh out of Yale he had married a Milton, one of the steamship, chemicals, and mining Miltons. Full professor at thirty. The promising young scholar had found himself a powerful patron in the foreign policy field, Orville Plummer (of the railroad Plummers). Rain just never seemed to fall on Kellicott's parade, until the early morning hours of a March day two years before.

PROFESSOR'S DAUGHTER SLAIN, the *Globe*'s headline read.

The body of Emily Kellicott, 26, was found early yesterday under a pile of snow in the parking lot of a mall on Lowell Parkway, Cambridge police said.

The victim, daughter of Harvard professor J. Alden Kellicott and his heiress wife, the former Susan Milton, had apparently been strangled to death. Her clothes were found in the snow beside the body, which bore lacerations.

Det. Sgt. Ray Harrigan said that there were preliminary indications of sexual assault, although final determination would not be possible until completion of the autopsy.

Harrigan said that while there were no suspects at present, investigations were continuing and Cambridge police had several promising leads. The dead woman was a Wellesley dropout who was said to have led a troubled life.

Her address was given as 37 Standish Lane, Cambridge, which was her parents' address. The president of Harvard, I happened to know, lived on the next block.

The story in the *Boston Herald* added nothing substantial to the account, although the tabloid made a good deal more of the beautiful-heiress angle and had dug up her yearbook portrait from Buckingham, Browne & Nichols School. Emily had been a pleasant-looking girl, if you could judge by the photograph, but not a beauty.

Plenty was missing from the stories. What was she doing in the parking lot at that hour? What was troubled about her life? What kind of lacerations did her body bear? Where? From what kind of instrument? Was her purse found? Was anything gone from it? Did she have a car? Where was it? Were bloodstains found in it? What were "preliminary indications of sexual assault"? What kind of assault? How long had she been dead? Had she been missing from home? How long?

Very likely the police didn't have the answers to some of those questions. Another cop had pointed out Sergeant Harrigan to me once; the joke was that he had been promoted to detective because he wasn't bright enough to fill out a parking ticket. But the reporters ought to have tried to plug the holes in their stories,

particularly the *Herald*'s man. When you worked for
Rupert Murdoch, you didn't let go of a murdered
"socialite beauty" until you had milked the last line of
copy out of her. And yet the second-day stories added
little to the first ones. A "sexual assault" of some
unspecified type had indeed occurred; the wounds to
some unspecified part of her body appeared to have been
made with a knife; the medical examiner estimated the
body had been lying unnoticed in its snowbank for
twenty-four hours or so.

The third-day stories added only that services would
be private, and the useful information that investigations
were continuing. There were no stories on the fourth or
fifth days, or after that. Their absence was hardly sur-
prising. I could almost see Professor Kellicott running
into the *Globe*'s publisher at the St. Botolph Club, and
the two of them agreeing on how painful all this was to
the poor girl's mother. The *Herald* might have been a
little tougher to reach through the old boys' network,
but at Kellicott's level everybody is acquainted with
everybody else, or knows someone who is. In conse-
quence we were for once spared the normal rooting
around in the victim's "troubled" past, and the pop-
sociological analyses of rebellious youth or whatever she
had been, and the stories prodding the police for inac-
tion, and the anniversary pieces every year until all
involved got tired of the mystery.

And so my days of poking around in the library had
brought nothing to the surface but two anomalies, two
breaks in the pattern of a phenomenally successful life.
Kellicott had left his parents out of his *Who's Who* entry,
and his older daughter had been murdered. Neither avenue looked terribly promising, but one of them led to
Sharon, which is in the Berkshire Mountains of northwest Connecticut. And the weather in Cambridge was

so hot that the asphalt gave under your weight. And Hope Edwards would be attending a conference in Stockbridge, which is in the Berkshire Mountains of southwestern Massachusetts. Hope Edwards is my lady and my love, even if I have to share her. Today was Wednesday and tomorrow was Thursday, the first day of the conference.

2

ONE OF MY FEW EXTRAVAGANCES IS MY CAR. IT'S AN
eight-year-old tan-colored Datsun that looks right at
home in Cambridge. Eight years of Cambridge residential
parking permits, the mark of the old-timer, clutter up
the left-hand side of the rear window. Rust is rotting
away the rocker panels and the bottoms of the doors. A
crack runs along the bottom of the windshield. The fend-
ers are chipped, bent, and dented. The upholstery used
to be sort of reddish, but the sun has long since bleached
it to a pale, unhealthy pink. Paper napkins, discarded
notebooks, old books, and nonbiodegradable trash from
Burger King and McDonald's cover the seats and floors.
Most of this optional equipment was left in place by the
car's previous owner, a divinity school student who sold
it to me for four hundred dollars three years ago, after
the steering gave out. He also left me his bumper stickers, which identified me as a friend of whales and an

enemy of war. This may have overstated the case slightly, but it was close enough for government work.

No thief was likely to bother hot-wiring the old junker, even though Greater Boston is the car-theft capital of America. After all, how could he know that the motor and the drivetrain and everything else you couldn't see were either new or rebuilt or perfectly maintained by the guys at MacKinnon Motors? That the aging clunker with the bad case of body cancer would keep on going at nearly forty miles to the gallon as long as you wanted it to? That the old AM radio with one knob missing was camouflage for a hidden CD player? The only thieves that ever bothered me were the worst ones of all, the ones with a license to steal, the companies that write auto insurance in Massachusetts.

Thursday afternoon the car started at the first touch, as always, and I headed toward the Mass Pike. For the first fifty miles or so going west from Boston, the pike goes through scenery that is about as dull as you can find in New England. The solution is to run up the windows, switch on the air-conditioning, turn Julie London on barely loud enough to hear, settle the speed at sixty, and, honey, as the song says, "let your mind roll on." What it mostly rolled on about was Hope Edwards, who was giving the keynote speech as well as leading several workshops at the annual meeting of the Massachusetts Bar Association. We were both card-carrying members of the American Civil Liberties Union, but she was also director of its Washington office. A lobbyist for criminals, as Ed Meese used to say. You would have thought he'd be grateful that somebody as smart as Hope was looking out for him and his pals.

Hope was as good-looking as she was smart, which seemed an unfair helping of blessings for one person to have, but that was only the beginning. She made good money herself, and was married to a Washington lawyer who made even more, and had two handsome small boys and a beautiful twelve-year-old daughter, and a big town house overlooking Rock Creek Park, and she was a champion sculler for the Potomac Boat Club, and she had an easy, outgoing way that made everybody either like or love her. And why she wasted as much as two minutes of her life on me, God knows, but there it was. Maybe she needed a dark side; certainly I needed a light one.

The farther west I drove on the pike, the prettier the countryside got. In the heavy heat each leaf and blade of grass and cow and high, white cloud stood still. Only the cars moved, roaring through the sun-stunned landscape. And one of them was carrying Dumb Tom Bethany to his sole and only true love, as I would admit to myself but never aloud.

"Oh, that's right, that's right, yes," I was saying when the phone rang, making it no longer right.

Hope reached out for the phone and answered it the best she could. "Uh-huh," she said. "Uh-huh, uh-huh. Uhn-uhn, huhn-uhn." Then she arranged matters so that she could broaden her vocabulary and said, "I'm afraid I'm bushed, Larry. I'll have to talk to you tomorrow." The instant she hung up she burst out laughing.

"What's so funny?" I said.

"Just something he said."

"What?"

"Nothing."

"Tell me or I'll hold my breath until I die."

"He wanted to know what I was eating."

Before I could deal with that properly, Hope attacked with the speed of a mongoose, tickling me till I could do nothing but laugh, and so I tickled her back, and there we were, rolling to escape each other like a pair of nine-year-olds. The odd thing is that I'm not ticklish with anyone else and neither is she. We are too dignified, to use a word no longer used. Too uptight, people say now. After a while we lay back on the pillows, laughed out. I reached for the phone and disconnected it.

"I looked in on your speech," I said. "When you were talking about *Arizona* vs. *Youngblood*."

"Mishandling evidence," she said. "Here, let me show you."

"I liked watching you."

"Hmm," she said into the side of my neck.

"Massachusetts bar. Whole roomful of men, hundreds. Made me feel good. You know why?"

"Mmm."

"Because I looked into their hearts, and every single male heterosexual in the room wanted to tickle you after the show. But none of them would except me, and they'd envy the shit out of me if they knew."

"I envy the shit out of you, too, and you know what I envy about you guys? Specifically?"

She made me forget for a while all about the sad part—that I had had to slip unobtrusively into the back of the hall instead of sitting in the front row as the guest of the featured speaker. Hope was a public lady, and it was public knowledge that she was married, or at least it was in a crowd of lawyers. So she had left a duplicate key to her room with me, and I had only looked in on the speech briefly. Then I went to her room and waited there for her. She would have made her excuses as soon after the talk as she gracefully could, and Larry, whoever he was, would have figured what the hell, why not wait a while and ring the room? All she can say is no.

Which she had to him, but not to me. After a long

and leisurely time we lay side by side, just touching along the length of our bodies.

"Driving down to Sharon and back tomorrow?" Hope asked.

"Ummh."

"Good. Two nights here, then."

And we lay there silent for a while more, until she said into the darkness, "Sharon is where Bill Buckley is from. Did you know that?"

"No, I didn't. Is there a shrine or something?"

"No, so you can't be going there for that. And you don't have any Republican friends. So why are you going?"

I was able to tell her everything, because she's the person I trust with everything. The only person.

"It's a dumb idea," Hope said when I told her about Markham's plan to name Kellicott. "All the Vance and Muskie people will be shooting at him because he was Brzezinski's mole at State."

"Sure it's dumb. But they're not paying me this outrageous price for political advice."

"When I get back to Washington I can ask around about Kellicott. If you want."

"Would you?"

And then, since Hope had a 7:30 breakfast meeting, we left a call for 6:00. That way, we figured, we would have time for a good long shower or something.

At 7:25 Hope was out the door, looking cool and businesslike and slightly remote, and not a bit the way she had looked a half an hour earlier. I took my time dressing, and only left the room after I had checked to be sure there were no ACLU lawyers hanging around the hall. Then I walked out of the inn, trying to look like an ACLU lawyer myself. It was the Red Lion Inn, a huge, sprawling hotel built in the days when trains brought rich New Yorkers up to summer in the Berkshires of western Massachusetts. The coolness of the night still hung on at quarter till eight. The lawyers weren't around yet to enjoy it, but two old ladies were already seated in the rocking chairs that ran the length of the inn's veranda. The scene wouldn't have been much different a century before. The Mauve Decade was a miserable time to be poor, but a wonderful time to be rich. Maybe these things go in hundred-year cycles, and Reagan was nothing but a historical imperative.

My car was parked conspicuously in a line of Saabs and Mercedes-Benzes and Porsches, a mutt among show dogs. Fuck all of you, was my reaction, at least I didn't steal for mine. An illogical and possibly even an unfair reaction, I know, but I can't help that. I have met the enemy often enough, and generally he ain't us. Generally he drives a Mercedes and stops at places like the Red Lion.

To get away from the inn, and the thought that Hope was having breakfast there but not with me, I drove down Route 7 to the McDonald's outside Great Barrington. When on the road I give my breakfast business to McDonald's, as the most intellectual of the fast-food chains. Who else sets out free copies of the local paper? And in this case the local paper was the *Berkshire Eagle*, an honest, workmanlike product that the chains haven't got around to swallowing yet.

Below Great Barrington down to the Connecticut line, to judge by the signs, the principal local industry was people selling their antiques to one another. The locals had evidently discovered the economic equivalent of a perpetual motion machine. On into Connecticut the antique shops thinned out somewhat. Here and there were modest houses, for the support troops, but the trend was toward million-dollar estates sitting well back from the road, shaded by trees way too big to get your arms around. The owners had to be beyond the necessity of going to the office every day, since New York City was a hundred miles to the south. Presumably they were the kind of people, as Hope describes them, who get money in the mail.

Sharon, Kellicott's hometown, had almost the air of a New England village restored by the Rockefellers to its original appearance. But not even the Rockefellers could restore the giant trees that must have shaded the entire village green before the Dutch elm blight hit. One or two huge elms remained, but the rest of the green was planted with maples no more than forty years old. I knew about tree age because till I went away to college and never came back, I had to cut wood to help get us through the north-country winters.

The white houses that stood around the green dated from the late 1700s or early 1800s. I'm not as good on houses as I am on trees; house ages I could tell because a number of them had the dates above the front doors. The town hall, a one-story brick building, seemed to be of more recent manufacture. The woman behind the counter in the town clerk's office gave me directions to where the Kellicotts once lived, the two parents being now dead. Since the clerk was a woman of a certain age, as the French say, and it seemed to be about the same age as Kellicott's, I asked her if she had gone to school with him.

"Jeff was a couple of grades ahead of me," she said.

"Jeff?" I asked.

"That's what he called himself in those days. Stood for Jeffrey, I imagine, but I'm just guessing. None of us knew him too well. He only stayed at Sharon Center School for the first few grades and then he went to Indian Mountain."

"What's that?"

"School for the hilltoppers, over in Lakeville. Like the prep schools, only they start younger." I got directions from her to Indian Mountain School, too. Then I asked if I could have a look at the deed to the Kellicott property.

"There isn't any Kellicott property. They lived on the Milton place."

"Susan Milton?" I asked, remembering the maiden name of Kellicott's wife.

"Well, her father's really. Leffingwell Milton. Not Little Leffingwell, the son that has the place now. Big Leffingwell. The old man who died."

"How did it happen that the Kellicotts lived on the Milton place?"

She looked at me as if I had asked a dumb question. "He drove for the Miltons."

"Who did?"

"Mike Kellicott did. Jeff's dad."

"How about his mom?"

"Nobody ever knew her. From what I understand, she died in childbirth with Jeff."

I went next to the probate office, across the hall. There I learned that Michael Kellicott had left everything he had to his son, Jephthah Alden Kellicott. The will superseded an earlier will in which he had left everything to his beloved wife, Catherine Wynsocki Kellicott. The legal boilerplate gave no clue to the size of the estate; presumably nothing much was involved beyond furnishings, personal effects, and maybe a few bucks in a bank account somewhere.

Leffingwell Milton's will was another matter. It went on for sixteen pages of bequests, codicils, trusts, trustees, etc. It was the will of a man with vast and complex business interests, and firm opinions about his heirs. Big Leffingwell, it seemed, had regarded Little Leffingwell as an idiot—or at least as a man who was incompetent to handle money.

The junior Leffingwell got the two-hundred-acre family homestead in Sharon, true enough. But the will went on to read:

"All the rest, residue and remainder of my estate, both real and personal, of every nature and wherever situate, of which I may die seized or possessed, including without limitation, all property acquired by me or to which I may become entitled after the execution of this Will, and all property herein attempted to be disposed of, the disposition whereof by reason of lapse or other cause shall fail to take effect, I give, devise and bequeath to my Trustees hereinafter named, IN TRUST NEVERTHE-LESS, for the following uses and purposes hereinafter set forth."

These uses included the upkeep and operation of the Sharon estate. But the apparently unbreakable trust was administered by a Hartford law firm. Little Leffingwell, in effect, had been put on a lifelong allowance. The trust was also charged with taking care of his children, who would inherit equal portions of a third of the trust's principal as each turned thirty-five. If I had been Little Leffingwell, I would have interpreted this as meaning that the old son of a bitch trusted my little kids more than he trusted me.

His sister, Susan, and her husband, Alden Kellicott, came out a lot better. Her trust fund amounted to two thirds of the estate, as compared with her brother's untouchable one third. She had immediate limited access to her two thirds of the trust, and had gained total control of the money at the age of forty. She was now, I knew, forty-nine. Kellicott, for his part, had inherited outright "the sum of $2,000,000 (two million dollars) to dispose of as he may see fit." My guess was that the old man saw the income from two million as barely sufficient to raise his son-in-law above the poverty line and give him a measure of psychological independence.

My further guess, pretty nearly amounting to a certainty, was that Little Leffingwell would hate his brother-in-law's guts. So naturally I called him up to see about a meeting, but he turned out to be in the middle of a month's fishing at his lodge in northern Quebec. The lodge was phoneless. That's the way it goes, often enough.

But I drove out to the Milton house anyway, to have a look at the place where Kellicott grew up. Before turning into its driveway, I pulled up along the blacktop country road and inspected the estate. The main house was a three-story brick building, weathered to a soft red. The roof was slate. A four-car garage with a cupola on top stood off to one side, all four doors open. Two of the bays were empty. Another held a 1956 Ford pickup that looked to be in excellent shape for its years; in the last was a new and shiny Jeep-type vehicle from Japan.

Like the house, the trees and plantings had been in place a very long time. The fences were made of stones cleared from the fields. Along the road, a tangle of brambles and bushes almost hid the fences from view. Large maples grew between the fence line and the roadside. The fields behind were unmowed, a tangle of midsummer wildflowers. Far beyond were barns and other fields, with brown and white cattle resting in the shade of the large trees that stood here and there. A standard hardware-store mailbox stood by the side of the road, with no name on it. Presumably the mail carrier knew who lived there.

I drove down the graveled driveway and parked in front of the house. No one came to the door, although I could hear the bell ringing inside the house. I could see the front hall through the narrow windows that ran up both sides of the front door. The general impression was of brass and leather and waxed mahogany and expensive wallpaper and striped or flowered upholstery. I heard footsteps on the gravel drive and turned to see a man in his sixties, carrying an edging tool.

"All gone," he said. "Mrs. M's in the city. Mr. M's off fishing in Canada with the kids."

"No fishing around here?"

"Oh, sure. There's a good stream right on the property, just this side of that rise. I been known to take a dozen or more brookies out of it, after a good rain."

"Can you work a fly in all that brush?"

"Oh, hell, no. Only way to get 'em out of there is worms. Couple of split buckshot and let the high water carry your bait down into the holes under the bank. And even then the sons of bitches'll hang your line up on a root half the time."

He paused a moment. "Up there where he goes," he went on, "the fish practically jump in the canoe with you. According to what they say, anyway."

"Some life," I said. "Actually, I wasn't looking for the Miltons, anyway. Actually, they told me the Kellicott place was out around here. Mike Kellicott?"

"Kellicott? He died in '79."

"Yeah, well, I knew he was dead. I just wanted to see the house."

"Just past the bend on the road, on your left. Not much to see, and I ought to know. I live there now."

"Thanks."

"I wouldn't have thought anybody even remembered old Mike Kellicott after all this time."

"I was just going to drive by, get an idea. I'm doing a magazine story on Alden Kellicott."

"I still can't get used to that Alden. I know he calls himself that now, but he was always Jeff around here. He's the one told me about those fish up in Canada, long time back."

"He used to go up there?"

"Oh, yeah, sure. Big Leffingwell practically raised Jeff like his own son."

"Already had a son, didn't he?"

"Well, yeah. He had little Leffingwell, that's up in Canada now."

"But he liked Jeff better?"

"Jeff done all right for himself. Put it that way."

The gardener had started to wonder who I was and whether he should be talking to me. It was time to move along.

Kellicott's childhood home turned out to be a two-story stucco cottage. Its walls were the color of wet cement. The trim was dark green, almost black. The house stood in the shade of several large hemlocks, and it probably smelled perpetually of mildew inside. Grass tried to grow in the yard, but there wasn't enough sun for it to do well. Kellicott had had to go elsewhere to find his place in the sun.

I couldn't see that there was much more to be gained from looking at the dreary little cottage, and so I drove the few miles to the school that the town clerk had mentioned. The Indian Mountain School receptionist had me wait in a sort of living room outside the headmaster's office while he finished with a phone call. I was glancing over the various awards and trophies on the wall when I came across the name "Jephthah A. Kellicott" as the 1952 winner of something called the Triangle Prize.

"Mr. Bethany?" a voice behind me said. "Hi, I'm Judd Baxter."

I turned to find a surprisingly young man, probably

around thirty-five, dressed for tennis and tanned to match. He wanted to be helpful, but the school didn't keep records that old, as far as he or his secretary knew. Although this was only his second year in the job, actually. Maybe I should try old Mr. Dooley, who was headmaster back then and still lived right down the road, on Lake Wononscopomuc. Evan Dooley.

"What do you give the Triangle Prize for?" I asked.

"Academics, sports, and character," the young headmaster said. "By vote of the faculty. It's our top prize."

I found the retired headmaster splitting wood outside a small house on the shore of a large lake. He was working slowly and carefully, getting the job done little by little. He looked pretty good for a man in his eighties, which Baxter had told me he was. When I stated my business he set aside his splitting maul willingly enough and invited me inside. An old springer spaniel on a couch opened his eyes just long enough to dismiss me as uninteresting, and went back to sleep again. His old master looked over my all-purpose letter of authorization from Alden Kellicott, and seemed equally unimpressed.

"I don't know how much help I can be to you, Mr. Bethany," he said. "It's been a long time."

"You do remember Professor Kellicott?"

"Oh, yes. Jeff was one of the brightest boys we ever had. He did well at everything. Sports, extracurricular activities. A good many of the students looked up to him."

"Popular with the faculty, too?"

"We voted him the Triangle Prize."

"What was the vote?"

"The actual vote? You need that for your story?"

"Probably not. I just like to get a feel for my subjects."

"Well, I don't remember what the vote was."

"How did you vote, yourself?"

"I don't think I'll remember that, either." Mr. Dooley took a sip of the iced tea he had brought both of us before I had started asking my questions. Then he looked at me with the disapproving stare that had no doubt unsettled hundreds of schoolboys. It unsettled me.

"I was in the school business forty years," he said. "A good many of my boys have done quite well by themselves. Actors, politicians, champion athletes one or two of them, one fellow won the Nobel Prize in chemistry. The man who produces the boxing films, what are they called?"

I shrugged. I didn't know, either.

"Over the years I imagine I've read a couple of dozen magazine stories about former students of mine, and not one of those reporters ever came all the way up here to interview the headmaster the boys had in the ninth grade."

Neither of us was fooling the other, and I decided to stop trying. "Mr. Dooley," I said, "I'll bet you voted for Jeff Kellicott for the Triangle Prize and I'll bet you held your nose when you did it."

"I don't know why you'd think that."

"Let me tell you about a conversation we might've just had, but didn't. Here goes your part. I'd be delighted to help you, Mr. Bethany. I could never forget Jeff. He was one of the finest boys we ever had. A terrific athlete and scholar. A natural leader. The faculty voted him our top prize."

"I said all those things."

"But I had to drag them out of you, and you qualified every one."

Dooley remained stubbornly silent, and so I knew I was on solid ground. It was coming to me that he was something I didn't run across often: a man of uncompromising, old-fashioned integrity. No doubt I wouldn't agree with him on most things, any more than I'd agree with Barry Goldwater. But I could count on what they said being what they really thought. If, that is, they chose to say anything at all.

"Do you keep up with politics, Mr. Dooley?" I asked.

"I do. I was treasurer of the Republican Town Committee till I gave it up last year."

"Do you think Senator Markham's going to the White House?"

"I wouldn't want to see it, but that's the way the polls are running right now."

"Then let me tell you something I hope you'll want to keep confidential once you've heard it."

The old headmaster nodded, and I went on.

"Alden Kellicott is likely to be our next secretary of state."

"That would be a mistake," Mr. Dooley said.

"I thought you might think so," I said, and did something I've never done before. I told him exactly who I was working for, and what I had already found out, and what I hoped still to find out. I also told him how Phil Jeffers would feel if he knew I had leaked the name of Markham's candidate for secretary of state to a former Republican official. Mr. Dooley listened till I was done. Then he closed his eyes for such a long time that I thought he might have gone to sleep.

At last he opened them, and said, "What's the phone number of the Markham campaign headquarters?"

"Five-four-six, four-six hundred. Area code six-one-seven."

"What's the extension of this campaign-manager fellow, this Jeffers?"

"Six-oh-nine."

He picked up the phone, dialed Boston information, and asked for the number of the Markham campaign.

Cute old man. When that checked out, he dialed the campaign switchboard and asked for extension 609. In a moment he nodded, apparently satisfied with the way the extension had been answered. "Yes, you can help me," he said to whoever had answered the phone. "If I wanted to mail something to Mr. Jeffers, how would I address it?"

I admired the way he had worked out to get the address without actually saying he intended to send Jeffers anything. Which would have been a lie, of course. Mr. Dooley listened to the answer to his hypothetical question, said thank-you, and hung up.

"I don't remember the address," I said, before he could ask. "But it's off Milk Street, used to be Axel, Shearman's Boston office."

"I'm satisfied," Mr. Dooley said, and began to talk.

Jeff Kellicott and Leffingwell Milton II had come to Indian Mountain in 1947, when they were both nine. For the first two years they were day students; from then on young Leffingwell was a boarding student, while Kellicott remained a day student. The senior Milton had become worried about his son's poor grades, and thought the boy would do better as a boarder.

"Did he?" I asked.

"Not really. They seldom do."

"How were Kellicott's marks?"

"He was the first in the school right from the start, every year."

"Do you have school buses?"

"We didn't then."

"How did the two of them get to school?"

"In the Miltons' station wagon."

"Who drove them?"

"Sometimes Mrs. Milton, but she was generally sick in the mornings. Most of the time it was Jeff's father."

"What was the matter with Mrs. Milton?"

"Ginny liked her cocktails."

"Where would the boys ride?"

The old headmaster looked puzzled.

"Up front with Jeff's father or in the back?" I asked. "Or maybe Jeff up front and the other boy in the back?"

"Both up front, I imagine. I don't really remember, but any other way would have looked peculiar, wouldn't it?"

"I don't know, really. I don't move in those circles, so I'm just trying to get a sense of how things fit together. Did Mrs. Milton ever drive Jeff later on, when her own son was a boarder?"

"I don't really know. Actually I never saw who brought him to school after Leff became a boarder, now that you mention it. Jeff would show up every morning from the direction of the barns. I always assumed he had his father drop him off down the road."

"Ashamed of his father, you think?"

"Maybe. Boys that age get odd notions."

"Who paid his tuition?"

"Leff Milton Senior paid. One check for both boys."

"How did they get along?"

"The boys? They got along beautifully, as far as anyone could tell."

"Far as anyone could tell? You think there was maybe something else going on, though?"

"Just a feeling I had. Nothing solid to it."

"On the surface what did it look like? Did they hang around together?"

"Quite a bit, yes. Jeff was one of those boys who's very self-assured, old for his age. Always a little bit aloof and independent. Other boys are drawn to that. They wanted him to like them."

"Did he?"

"Not the way they wanted, no. He was always pleasant, always nice to everybody. But a little remote, you know. No real best friend, or even close friends. Although you'd see him more often with Little Leff than with anyone else."

"Was Little Leff popular?"

"Alone, Leff would have been in the middle of the pack. Not the most popular, not unpopular either. But being with Jeff made him popular. Leff and Jeff, the kids called them. Like Mutt and Jeff. I suppose nobody remembers Mutt and Jeff anymore."

I nodded to show that I did, at least. "Apparently Kellicott was good at sports," I said. "How about the Milton boy?"

"Potentially better than Jeff. You have to understand that neither of them was a great natural, the kind of athlete that only comes along now and then. In terms of ability they were probably in the middle, or a little above. But Leff didn't have the fire and Jeff did. Jeff made himself into a standout."

"That the way it was in the classroom, too?"

"Oh, no. Leff's aptitude was pretty well below the middle there, and Jeff was the best student we ever had. He was one of those people who can read something once and never forget it. One of those trick memories."

"Is memory enough?"

"At our level, it pretty much is. But we've had one or two other students with photographic memories and they didn't do as well as Jeff. He had an amazingly quick mind, too. He'd grasp a concept while you were still in the middle of explaining it."

"Well, you know, so far I can't see why you think it would be such a mistake to make him secretary of state."

"It was a mistake to give him our Triangle Prize, too,

40

but you couldn't not give it to him. I hope it won't be like that this time."

"Why was it a mistake, though? He fulfilled all the requirements for the prize, didn't he?"

"That's it exactly. He fulfilled them. You felt he was doing all the things he was doing not because he wanted to, but because he knew you wanted him to. You felt he was using you. He was always respectful, always pleasant, always polite, and there was nothing you could ever put your finger on. But you always felt the way you do with a waiter, you know? That he's only smiling because he's learned you get bigger tips that way."

"And maybe because he knows he just spit in your soup, too," I said.

"Exactly," the old headmaster said. "That's exactly the way Jeff made you feel."

"He's better at it now," I said. "Or maybe he's changed."

"He may be better, but I doubt if he's changed. In my experience, the person you are at twelve is pretty much the person you're going to be, under the surface at least, for the rest of your life. That's why I'm telling you things I'd normally keep confidential. Like that old cheating business."

"You haven't told me about any cheating business."

"I haven't? Well, perhaps I haven't. Short-term memory loss. Fortunately, most of the things I want to remember call for long-term memory."

Mr. Dooley was silent for a moment.

"It's forty years ago now, and you'd think everybody would have forgotten it," he continued. "Unimportant schoolboy stuff. But every time I see Leff I think about it, and I'd bet you he does, too. Not that either of us would ever mention it. I'd bet Jeff remembers it too, although I haven't seen him since Honors Day when he walked off with all the prizes. Funny thing, Leff didn't do nearly so well here, but he went on to take quite an interest in the school over the years. Even served a term on the board of trustees. That's something you see more than you might think. You take a boy who must have had a miserable time in school, you'd think he'd put it all behind him. But just as often as not he'll wind up as class agent, active in alumni affairs, annual giving, going to all the reunions. It's almost like they're trying to give themselves a second crack at school, to make a go of it this time around . . ."

"I gather the Milton boy was the one who cheated?" I prompted.

"I don't know, damn it. Never will know. Officially, the Kellicott boy was the one who did."

"What happened?"

"Well, it was when they were both day boys, living at home. Leff turned in a paper that was much better than he usually did—got a B, as I recall. Jeff turned in a paper that was worse than he ever did. Also a B. Wasn't just the grades that were the same. Whole sections of the papers were, too. Jeff admitted that he had copied from Leff."

"Wait a minute, Mr. Dooley, am I getting this straight? The smarter one, Jeff, copied from the dumber one, Leff?"

"That's right."

"What would be the point of that?"

"Jeff said he did it because he just got behind."

"Had he ever got behind before?"

"Nope. Nor after."

"Didn't he know that the teacher would be bound to spot it?"

"They had different teachers. Jeff was in an advanced English section. Covered roughly the same material and had the same writing assignments, but they read more in Jeff's section."

"How *did* the teacher spot it, then?"

"That was odd, too. Leff's teacher, in the regular section, was the one who caught it. Leff's paper mentioned a poem that Leff's teacher hadn't assigned, but Jeff's had. So the two teachers compared notes."

"What did the Milton boy say about it all?"

"Just that Jeff had helped him a lot with his paper, but hadn't really written it. It turned out they did their homework together a good deal of the time, with Jeff sort of being the teacher. That confused the whole thing even more, of course."

"But there's no confusion about Jeff turning in a paper that wasn't his?"

"Some confusion, yes. Jeff might have in effect written the paper Leff turned in. That's what Leffingwell Senior thought."

"Meaning that Jeff would have turned in a B paper that was essentially his and Leff would have turned in pretty much the same B paper as Jeff's. In which case Leff was the one who cheated, and Jeff tried to cover for him."

"But why would Jeff have done such a thing?" Mr. Dooley asked. "He could have written a much better paper for himself. That's what has always baffled me."

"Supposing he had written his own A paper and helped Leff write a B paper. Probably nobody would have suspected anything."

"Why didn't he do that, then?" the headmaster asked.

"What if he intended to be caught?"

"I find that hard to believe."

"Or at the very least didn't care if he was caught, because he would be in a no-lose situation."

"He could easily have been expelled for plagiarism. That would have been quite a loss."

"It didn't happen, though, did it? What happened was that nobody believed that Jeff cheated, and everybody believed Leff did."

"I had my doubts. But no evidence."

"Mr. Milton didn't have any doubts. He thought his son had copied from the chauffeur's son, didn't you say?"

"He ranted and raved about it for a while, yes. Big Leff could be a very forceful man."

"A bully?"

"Some might say so. He certainly reduced Little Leff to tears that day. Told the boy he was going to be a boarder from then on, so he'd be forced to do his own homework for a change."

"Was Jeff there, too?"

"Oh, yes, I had all three of them in my office, Leffingwell Milton and the two boys. Very unpleasant scene."

"Jeff Kellicott's father wasn't there?"

"I never really knew Mike Kellicott. Leff Milton paid the bills, and Jeff's father never really entered the picture."

"What did Jeff say during this meeting?"

"He took all the blame and did his best to clear Leff. Said he hadn't helped Leff hardly at all with his paper. Said he was sorry he cheated and was ready to accept whatever the punishment was."

"What was it?"

"Nothing. I had no real evidence that Jeff had written Leff's paper for him. And if he had, I couldn't very well punish Jeff for plagiarizing himself. To this day, I don't really know what happened. I just suspect."

"Suspect what?"

"That Jeff planned it all. What I don't know is why."

I didn't know why, either, although I had one or two notions about it. Freud tells us that the result achieved is apt to be the result intended, and even Freud can't be wrong all the time. In this case the results achieved had been to drive Big Leff and Little Leff apart, while at the same time bringing Big Leff and the Kellicott boy closer together. Would a schoolboy be capable of thinking up and then carrying out such a complicated, sophisticated scheme?

"Do you still see anything of Little Leff?" I asked the old man.

"Not really," he said. "While I was still at school I saw quite a bit of him at board meetings and so on. And then after my retirement I'd occasionally run across him at the little country club we have over in Sharon. But I gave up tennis a couple of years ago, when I turned eighty."

"Did he ever talk about Kellicott?"

"Constantly."

"In what terms?"

"Admiration. Gratitude."

"Gratitude for what?"

"What he's done for Susie."

"Is that Susan Milton?"

"Yes, Leff's sister. She was a handful when she was young, and I guess Jeff took her on and steadied her down. God knows her father couldn't do anything with her."

"What was the problem?"

"Partly the bottle, I gather. Like her mother, poor soul. She was always—Susie was, not her mother—getting fired from schools and disappearing with inappropriate people and attempting suicide. That sort of thing."

"Did Big Leff feel gratitude, too?"

"Oh, he was delighted over the marriage. He used to say that buying Jeff an education was the smartest investment he ever made."

"Did he admire Jeff, too?"

"I doubt if Big Leff ever admired anybody except himself. This is going to sound funny, but he wasn't really bright enough to understand that Jeff was brighter than him."

"Doesn't sound funny at all," I said, and it didn't. To think you're smart when you're not, you have to be really stupid or really rich. Big Leff seemed to have qualified on both counts.

I thanked Evan Dooley for his help, meaning every word of it, and headed a mile or so down the road for the next stop on Kellicott's path upward, Hotchkiss School. It turned out to be a collection of undistinguished-looking brick dormitories and halls that barely missed looking like the buildings at a state mental hospital. The place was maintained a little better, though. And the windows, while they lacked curtains, also lacked bars.

I asked directions from a group of summer students who seemed to be majoring in competitive dressing, and found my way to the administrative offices. The assistant headmaster who finally agreed to see me was totally unimpressed by Kellicott's letter authorizing Hotchkiss to show me his records and extend all other courtesies. The furthest he would go was to permit me to examine the yearbooks in the school library, and even then he took no chances. He escorted me there, and instructed the librarian to limit my browsing to the yearbook in question.

"I wish we could help you more, Mr. Bethany," he said in a friendly way that fooled neither the librarian nor me. "Fact is, though, the law is pretty darned strict on the privacy of student records. But I'm sure Harriet would be glad to show you the 1956 yearbook, not that we're a public library of course. That should be enough to give you a darned good overview of Dr. Kellicott's career at Hotchkiss." I thought of the young headmaster at Indian Mountain, who hadn't been any more helpful than this turkey, really. But two guys can say pretty much the same thing, and still you can tell right off which one is the asshole and which one isn't. Style is substance.

Actually, the yearbook probably did give as darned good an overview of Kellicott's Hotchkiss career as his records would have. He had won most of the available prizes. Although he didn't strike me as particularly well-constructed for contact sports, he had lettered in football and hockey, as well as tennis. He had been president of the student council, editor of the school newspaper, and a member of the cum laude society.

I returned the book to Harriet, who was in the process of closing up shop, and went back out into a day that remained hot. At a little after five the sun was still burning down strongly out of a blue sky, with high, white, puffy clouds here and there. I had parked in the shade, but the shade had moved. The car seat was so hot that I had to take my weight off it a time or two and let the air in under before I could sit down without hurting.

Hope's room at the Red Lion was air-conditioned, though, and cool enough to make you uncomfortable without clothes on. This forced us to stay under the covers until it was time for dinner. By then the heat had broken outside. We drove a few miles out of town and ate bad food at a restaurant called Trumbull's Taverne. The "e" should have tipped us off. The menus opened out to the size of a *Boston Globe* at full extension and the dishes had names like "Priscilla's Deep-Dish Apple Dowdy." All the esses were written as efs, but at least they had Baff Ale on tap.

Afterward we drove for miles on some county road until we found a lonely spot to park, and then we did something we did whenever we got the chance. Why, I don't know. I'm just reporting. We necked like teenagers for an hour or more under the crescent moon. We did everything you can do short of going all the way, and then we drove back to the inn and did that, too.

Next morning, Saturday, I drove Hope to Worcester, where she was catching a flight home. Along the way, I told her what I had learned about Kellicott.

"How old was he when this business with the plagiarized paper happened?" she asked.

"Ten, around in there."

"That young, you think he was capable of setting the Milton boy up so his father would send him away from home to be a boarder?"

"No, I don't think he could have predicted the boarder part. It was just a lucky accident that Little Leff got moved out of the way."

"So young Jeff could move in on the old man?"

"He seen his opportunities, and he took 'em."

"What part wasn't an accident, then?" Hope asked.

"The part that couldn't have been. Jeff turning in the same paper he had helped Little Leff write."

"Little Leff. Poor little rich kid."

"Sure, he was in a double bind. What was he supposed to say? My best friend helped me with my paper and then turned in the same paper himself? Certain drawbacks to that, but what other choice did he have? He was stuck with the truth."

"And the truth was unbelievable," Hope said.

"Right. The only conclusion that Big Leff could possibly draw, remembering here that it doesn't look like he was any brighter than Little Leff, was that his boy had copied from the chauffeur's boy."

"Do you really think a ten-year-old kid could have plotted all that out?"

"Not really, no. Maybe he just thought it was a joke. Maybe he just got tired of helping his dumb pal with his homework. But I think he thought it through enough to know there was no real downside for him."

"And no upside for Little Leff?"

"That part I doubt. I'd bet that part was unconscious or subconscious, whatever. Just a kind of an underlying understanding that anything that made Little Leff look bad would probably make Jeff look good."

"I imagine you're right," Hope said. "Guys like Kellicott seem more conniving than they really are, because their hearts are pure."

"That's deep, very deep. What does it mean?"

"Means that somebody like you looks at somebody like Kellicott and says, boy, is that a smart son of a bitch. He figures life out like a chess game, three or four moves ahead all the time."

"Doesn't he?"

"Not in quite such a calculating way, no. All it is, Kellicott only has one thing in his head. Getting to be secretary of state. So he looks at the entire world, everything, through that particular lens. Which socks should he wear? Where should he go to college? Who should he marry? No problem. He just checks off the boxes that will get him to the seventh floor of State the fastest."

"Doesn't he need a brain to know which boxes to check?"

"Not much of one. Those aren't tough choices to make. Anybody could figure out that a Yale degree is better than a CCNY degree, for instance, if what you want to be is secretary of state. What's that place where the swallows go?''

"Capistrano?''

"Okay, every one of those swallows knows the best way to Capistrano. That's a no-brainer.''

"Of course none of them could get into Yale," I said.

"I'm not saying Kellicott isn't smart," Hope said. "I'm just saying that guys like him can look a lot more brilliant and Machiavellian than they are. Same way those swallows look pretty bright, for birds. But they're just machines that are programmed to get to that bell tower by a certain date.''

"Still, I couldn't do it.''

"Sure you could, if you were a machine for becoming secretary of state. Look at Sully Shapiro and Robert Holton.''

One was a Democratic congressman from Ohio, the other had been deputy to one of Reagan's parade of national security advisers.

"Are they as close to it as Kellicott?''

"My guess is any one of the three could wind up with the job. I don't know Kellicott, but I do know the other two. And you're smarter than either of them.''

"I just lack that instinct for the bell tower, huh?''

"You have more interesting instincts, thank God. But you can be just as single-minded.''

"I was about wrestling, for years.''

"And other things. Whenever you get interested, you don't let go. You're interested in Kellicott, aren't you?''

"Yeah, I am. You know one of the things I found out in the library? Kellicott was one of the most active backers of the Olympic boycott.''

"So it's payback time?''

"No, that isn't it. What it is, he told me he had argued against the boycott. He didn't have to say that. He didn't have to say anything at all. I don't think we ought to have a secretary of state who lies when he doesn't have to."

"Actually," Hope said, "I think it's in the job description."

"It shouldn't be."

"I know. Look, I'll ask around in Washington next week. And you go see the ACLU guy up here, the head of our Boston office. He used to carry Kellicott's briefcase at State."

3

I MET TOBY INGERSOLL AT HIS OFFICE MONDAY MORNING. He was a round-faced, round-bellied young man wearing round glasses that needed polishing. His shoes needed no polishing, being sneakers. But they could have done with a scrubbing, or whatever you do with sneakers that have turned gray. He wore dark blue cotton socks, falling down, with clocks on them. I wouldn't have thought it was still possible to buy socks with clocks on them; maybe they had been in the family for a long time. Maybe his baggy gray flannels had been, too. Lately pleated pants seem to be coming back, but Ingersoll's pair, loose-cut, low-crotched, cuffed and untapered, hadn't been in style since before he was born. The rest of his fashion statement was a rumpled, button-down blue cotton shirt with the sleeves rolled up, and a four-dollar haircut.

I liked him immediately. I got the same feeling from

him that I had from Dooley, the old headmaster: not that he didn't give a damn what opinion people might have of him, but that he had never thought about the question at all. I would have bet he had lots of friends, and when he smiled, I wanted to be one of them.

"Dump that crap on the floor and sit down," he said after we shook hands. I cleared the papers off the red vinyl seat of a tubular steel kitchen chair and set them among the other piles of papers and books that already littered the floor.

"Hope says to tell you whatever you want to know," Ingersoll said. "Jesus, I'm in love with her, you know that? Been in love with her for years. Her and Susan Sarandon."

I hadn't yet said a word, hadn't even started on the smile the remark seemed to call for, when something changed in his face. What? Some tiny rearrangement of features? Denoting what? Sympathy? Sudden awareness that this particular line of chatter carried an emotional charge for this particular visitor? What signal had I given? How had he picked it up? Maybe it was an accident that he changed the subject just then, but I doubted it. Unsettling to think that someone could spot a nonexistent blush on your face.

"Anyway, anyway," he said. "How come you're interested in Alden?" That tiny change in expression came again, as if he had just read something on a Teleprompter I didn't know about. "Shit, it doesn't matter why," he said. "If you come from Hope, you're all right."

What the hell, I had already trusted a Republican headmaster with the campaign's big secret. I might as well trust the director of the American Civil Liberties Union's Boston office, especially since he probably already knew it from sensing my magnetic field or pulse rate or brain waves or whatever he did.

"I'm woodshedding him for Markham," I said. "Markham wants him for secretary of state."

If Ingersoll was surprised he didn't show it, and he had a face that showed every passing shower or sunbeam. "What do you need to know?" he said.

"Hard to say till I hear it," I said. "Everything, I guess. How did you meet him?"

The round fullness of Ingersoll's face made him look younger than he was. But he was old enough to have been a graduate student studying government under Professor Kellicott when Carter was elected president. And he followed his mentor down to Washington as his special assistant for the last two years of the administration.

"Best jobs in Washington for a young guy," Ingersoll said. "They used to call them private secretaries until they invented the typewriter and started to call women secretaries. Now they call them special assistants. A lot of it's briefcase-carrying, and note-taking, and follow-through. But you get to sit in on practically everything, and you absorb a lot of the boss's power, just by proximity. I learned a lot. Enough to make me want to get out of government and go to law school and sign up with the forces of the Antichrist."

"You learned that from Kellicott?"

"Him and others. Mainly Kellicott."

"Now Kellicott's going to be Christ," I said. "Vicar of Christ, anyway."

Ingersoll smiled. "Not many people remember that," he said. Alexander Haig called himself Christ's Vicar when he took over the State Department for Reagan. Kissinger, who had Haig for a gofer in the days of Richard Nixon, thought of himself as the Lone Ranger. Did Haig, in those gone, golden days with Tricky Dick, think of himself as Tonto? These are things we will never know.

"What kind of a secretary will Kellicott make?" I asked Ingersoll.

"I'd rather see somebody like Shapiro or Holton in there."

"Why?"

"Because Kellicott's a lot smarter than they are."

"That's bad, huh?"

"Sure. If a job's not worth doing, it's not worth doing well."

"Secretary of state's not worth doing?"

"Not under any president we've had in my lifetime. Well, maybe Carter for the first few months. Before Brzezinski had poured too much poison in his ear."

"Yeah, well, okay. I can put it in my report that Kellicott is twice as smart as all the other candidates. That ought to finish him off."

"I don't expect to finish him off."

"But you'd like to?"

"I suppose I would."

"Well, go ahead, then. Do your best."

As Ingersoll described it, special assistants are like valets in one sense: if they're going to be any use to the boss, he's got to let them get close enough to see him with his clothes off. Kellicott seemed to have had no qualms about dropping trou in front of his aide; in fact he apparently did it enthusiastically, as part of the younger man's education. Most of the things Ingersoll told me were the small, routine obscenities of a successful bureaucrat's life: taking credit for the work of your subordinates, suppressing bad news and punishing its bearers, grabbing turf from rivals while protecting your own, massaging the facts until they seemed to support the boss's preconceptions, making sure that the boss never spoke alone with any of your subordinates—or, insofar as possible, with any other human being but you.

All of this was routine stuff which he had probably absorbed as a graduate student at Harvard, watching the professors snap and snarl like starving razorbacks over what few crumbs came their way. One of Ingersoll's stories, though, showed a nastiness well beyond the normal.

It was during the Iranian hostage crisis, if anything lasting 444 days can be called a crisis. But life went on, and on that particular day the problem that had brought Kellicott and his young aide to the White House situation room was death squads in El Salvador. The President was there, and a bunch of other people, and the White House expert on Latin America, a man named Paul Lasker. Lasker was Kellicott's opposite number at the White House, and his greatest bureaucratic enemy.

"Kellicott had been trying to get Lasker fired for eighteen months," Ingersoll said, "but the guy kept hanging on. It was driving poor old Alden nuts. At the time of this particular meeting, the issue between them was aid to El Salvador. Lasker wanted to cut it off, and Kellicott wanted to continue it.

"Lasker had a plane waiting for him at Andrews to take him to Argentina or some damned place, but he kept it waiting and fought on till he got agreement to cut off aid. He finally asked for a show of hands and won it, six to two. And one of the six was the President. Lasker figured that locked it up, so he grabbed his bags and headed for Andrews.

"Alden hadn't had much to say up to that point," Ingersoll said. "But then he moved in. He never said a harsh word about Lasker. In fact you came away thinking Paul was a warm, woolly, huggy-bear kind of a guy. Except he should never have been allowed out of the nursery to play with the grown-ups.

"You've heard Alden talk, that great voice he has.

Deep, reassuring. Makes you want to be just as reasonable and sensible and pragmatic and practical as he himself is. It's the voice your father should have had.

"Took him twenty minutes, but he turned the thing around. The next show of hands was four to three for continuing aid, and the President was one of the ones who switched. So that was that, or so I thought in my youthful ignorance.

"On the way back to Foggy Bottom I congratulated Kellicott on his win. I still remember what he said. Said it was irrelevant, he had it fixed on the Hill so Congress wouldn't cut the aid anyway. The real victory would come tomorrow. And so it did.

"Next day Evans and Novak said in their column that the administration had decided to cut off aid to El Salvador. Lots of colorful and accurate details. Even had a rundown of the six–two vote. You see the beauty of it, of course?"

"Sure," I said. "Lasker had to be the leaker, since he was the only one who left early and didn't know that the final vote went the other way. I assume the real leaker was Kellicott?"

"Actually I was. Kellicott had me call them."

"How much longer did the poor guy last?"

"Lasker? A week after he got back from the Argentina trip he was named ambassador to Burkina Faso. You know what the capital of Burkina Faso is?"

"Ouagadougou."

"Vicar of Christ, now Ouagadougou," Ingersoll said. "What is this shit?"

"I'm like Kellicott. I've got a trick memory."

"Oh, yeah? I bet you don't know what the embassy staff does for excitement in Ouagadougou."

"That I don't know."

"Every Sunday they go over to the ambassador's residence and look down the well."

"Out of curiosity, what he had you do to Lasker, is that the kind of thing that made you leave the government?"

"Hell, no, I still do that kind of thing. What do you think I'm doing right now?"

"You got a point there."

"The point is who you do it to, and why. In government, a lot of the time you're doing it to the good guys, for bad reasons. Now I try to do it for good reasons, to the bad guys."

"You think what you've given me on Kellicott will do it to him?"

"Hell, no. It'll be a character recommendation."

"Well, if anything more comes to mind, call this number and leave a message for me, okay?" I scribbled the number of the Tasty on a piece of paper for him.

Ingersoll shoved it into a corner of the old blotter on his desk, along with a dozen other slips of paper. "The only other thing that comes to mind is nothing, really," he said. "But two or three years ago I saw him down in the Combat Zone, coming out of a dirty bookstore. Tell you the truth, I was kind of surprised."

"Which dirty bookstore?"

"The one across from the Black Cat Theater."

"You don't mind my asking, what were you doing in the Combat Zone?"

"I don't mind your asking. I was coming out of a suck-and-fuck flick, something with Georgina Spelvin. You know her?"

"Not personally. But I know her work."

It was only quarter till eleven, and so I headed from Ingersoll's cluttered office to the cluttered former office of Axel, Shearman to see if I could catch Phil Jeffers before he took off for a fancy lunch on somebody else's expense account. I found him in the fax room, shouting at a volunteer, a skinny kid who looked about eighteen.

"I'm sorry, Mr. Jeffers," the kid was saying. He was red and ashamed and embarrassed and about to cry. "I tried to follow the instructions Louise gave me but the machine just ate it."

"Don't try to blame Louise, you dumb shit. Jesus fucking H. Christ, do I have to do every fucking thing myself around this fucking place?"

"I'm sorry, Mr. Jeffers. I said I was sorry." Then the most awful thing the kid could probably imagine happened and his eyes overflowed in front of the four or five other staffers who were standing around, being glad they weren't him. He turned and ran from the room.

"Boy oh boy, are you a tough son of a bitch," I said, keeping my tone flat and my voice just loud enough so all the staffers could hear. "I would never dare mess with a tough son of a bitch like you, not in a million years."

"Oh, fuck you, Bethany," Jeffers said. "Let him go home to Mama. Politics ain't beanbag."

"Oh, no, politics is hardball. Politics is hot kitchens. If I was a newsmagazine you know what I would call you, Phil? I would call you hard-boiled. That's how they spell *bully*."

"Did you come over here to piss on my leg or to earn your goddamn money?"

"Both."

"Well, now you pissed on my leg. Come on into the office."

He was really mad when we got alone, not just the playact mad he had been with the kid. It showed in the way he closed the door behind us, slow and careful, testing that it was good and shut—overcompensating because he wanted to smash the son of a bitch home with all his strength. He sat down behind his desk without motioning me to sit down. I sat down anyway. When other people get mad I slow down instead of speed up, for some reason. I get cold instead of getting hot back at them. That's what had got Jeffers so mad out in the fax room, and it was what was getting him madder now. I waited patiently.

"I never met a pain in the ass as bad as you," he finally said. "What is this shit, you dump on me in front of my people?"

"Who were you dumping on the kid in front of?"

"Fuck the kid."

I sat and waited. Jeffers rubbed his jaw and looked at me, and looked out the window, and looked at me again. He picked up the phone. "Louise," he said, "send the Shure kid in, okay?"

Neither of us said anything else till the kid came in. His cheeks weren't wet anymore but his eyes were still red. "Jason," he said, "this is Tom Bethany. He's helping us out."

"How do you do, Mr. Bethany," the kid said, still sounding shaky. I nodded. Jeffers got up, went over to the kid, and put his arm around the boy's shoulders.

"Jason here is helping us out, too," he said, at first to me. Then he spoke to the boy. "I was a shit to you out there, Jason," he said. "You know it?"

"That's all right, Mr. Jeffers."

"I could say I'm under a lot of pressure and all kinds of shit like that, but that would be shit, too. I didn't have to be a shit and I didn't have to say what I did to you, and I'm sorry."

"Really, Mr. Jeffers, it's okay."

"Phil." The boy stood silent. "Come on, say it," Jeffers said. "Phil."

"Phil."

Jeffers smiled. He took his arm from around the boy's shoulders. He shook the boy's hand with his right hand while his left hand gripped the boy's thin forearm. "Friends?" he asked.

"Friends," said the boy. Now he was smiling, too.

Jeffers took him out the door, patted him on the shoulders, and loud enough for a couple of nearby people to hear, said, "Hey, I just had the rag on, okay? I'm sorry."

When we were alone again, I said, "What can I say? I was wrong. Actually you're a really nice guy."

"Bullshit to that, too. But I'm not a stupid guy. I don't stay mad. Now I got a friend instead of an enemy, cost me two minutes."

I sat there. I wasn't the friend he had. Let him come to me.

"What've you got on the professor?" he said after a minute.

I gave him the biographical stuff, all of which he knew except for the nature of Kellicott's original relationship to the Miltons.

"That's just stuff from old clippings," he said when I wound down. "That's all you got?"

"Well, he told me the 'J.' in his name stands for Jephthah," I said, pronouncing it as Kellicott had during our interview, with the "p" hard.

"Yeah?" he said, so I spelled it for him.

"It's 'p, h,' " I said. "Pronounced 'f.' When he was a kid he called himself Jeff."

"So?"

"So Jep might sound weird and you might want to go by your middle name, but what's wrong with Jeff?"

"Stop jerking me around. What else have you got?"

"He's a prick, Phil. He's a knife artist."

"Literally?"

"Not literally, no. Literally he's not a prick, either. Only the part of him that made him rich."

"That's no crime."

"I've been talking to a few people, Phil. The guy is a compulsive liar and he's paranoid and he's completely amoral. Probably a very smooth borderline sociopath, or maybe not so borderline."

"Hey, we're not looking for Mother Teresa here. We're looking for a secretary of state."

"Well, I just thought you'd be glad to know you're on the right track. Only bad thing I could come up with is he likes dirty books."

"Dirty books?"

"I got a guy saw him coming out of a dirty bookstore in the Zone."

"So? Jacking off's no crime."

"I guess it depends what you jack off to." And I set right off to the Combat Zone to find out.

The Black Cat Theater was playing a pirate movie called *Jolly Rogered*, starring Jolly. The bookstore across the street had no name, unless its name was XXX ADULT BOOKS VIDEOS XXX. The shop window had been painted over so that you couldn't see inside. I went in, hoping it was air-conditioned, and it was.

To the right of the door was a sort of cubicle, raised up so that the enormously fat man sitting in it could overlook the racks. He was doing paperwork at his desk, and barely bothered to glance up when I came in. The three or four customers didn't even do that much. Each man pretended he was alone, kept quiet, and minded his own business. Dirty bookstores are the last public places in America where good manners survive. Or almost.

"*This ain't a library,*" the fat man brayed. Even then the customers remained polite, pretending that no one had rudely raised his voice. And in fact the fat man had sounded bored, not angry. Like everybody else, I continued to paw through the picture books. Where I was, they had names like *Bottoms Up* and *Hershey Highways*. Other sections were devoted to cunnilingus, pregnant women, bondage and sadomasochism, overdeveloped mammaries, pedophilia, homosexuality, obese women, biracial couples, and fellatio. There was even a small section that catered to the unweaned, as far as I could tell. Who else would pay twelve bucks to look at breasts dribbling milk?

After I had checked the stock out pretty thoroughly, I went up to the fat man on his enclosed platform. "Got anything with kangaroos?" I asked.

"Huh?"

"Kangaroos."

"Kangaroos?"

"Right. You know, with pouches. I like pouches."

"Nah, we don't carry it. I doubt they make it. I never heard of it."

Once again, I was missing connections somehow. When I'm serious, people think I'm trying to be funny. And when I'm trying to be funny, they take it seriously.

"Just a little joke," I said.

"This is a bookstore, Jack," the fat man said.

"Oh, right. Well, actually, what I wanted was something else anyway. I wanted to ask, are you the manager?"

"Yeah, I'm the manager. Why?"

"Well, I was looking for this certain item I saw in here maybe three years ago."

"What item?"

"Probably you wouldn't recognize it from my description unless you were here then."

"Six years I been here, all right? Every book goes in and out of here, I know it."

"Well, it's not a book, that's the thing. It's this guy. Ever see him in here?"

The fat man looked at the photograph of Kellicott I had handed him and said, "What is this shit? You a cop or what?"

I slid a folded twenty-dollar bill across the raised counter toward him, keeping my hand firmly on it. That let him know I wasn't a cop; in his line of work the cash flow was to cops, not from them. His manner changed from uncertain confusion to hostility.

"You're not here to buy books, you better get out," he said.

"I don't want to know who he is," I said. "Just what kind of books he buys."

"Out."

A good idea came to me. "See, I already know who he is," I said. "He's a rich guy. You tell me what he reads, I'll give you his name." But the fat man was too stupid to see the blackmail possibilities in my good idea, which was probably why he was the manager of a porno bookstore instead of something higher in the organization, like a drug dealer or a loan shark.

"All right, asshole," he said. "You asked for it."

He reached under the counter to press a button. I heard it ring in the back, where you paid a quarter to watch a few seconds of a dirty movie in a dirty booth. A short, wide, strong black man with a lot of scar tissue around his eyes came out.

"Lou?" he asked the fat man.

"Asshole here won't leave," Lou said.

The man put his hand on my shoulder, which is a move that a wrestler deals with thousands of times over the years. I forced him to his knees and leaned into his wrist joint enough to make him scream. Now my fellow customers were paying attention. So was Lou.

I made the man turn over onto his face on the floor and ran my free hand over him. Once I had taken away the balisong butterfly knife he carried, I set him loose.

"I know a lot of shit like that," I told him. "Try me again and I'll break both your thumbs."

The man said nothing. Lou said nothing. I said to Lou, "You, you fat fuck, you sicced him on me."

Without giving Lou time to think that over, I grabbed a handful of the belly that strained his dingy T-shirt. I squeezed the fat as hard as I could and twisted it, like turning off a faucet. Another thing you develop in wrestling is a really strong grip. Now Lou screamed, too, which seemed only fair.

The sudden summer daylight was blinding when the Red Line train first came up out of the ground on its way over to Cambridge. Several convicts were leaning against the grid work of bars that covers the windows of the Charles Street Jail. One flashed a finger at the train as it rolled along the trestle nearly level with his third-floor window. Only a few sailboats were out in the boat basin, and those were under power, with their sails slack. There was no breath of wind. The air was heavy with lightning to come. But for the moment the sky was bright blue, except for a line of dark clouds off to the northwest. The train went underground again, once it had crossed the river over to the Cambridge side. I thought about what I had learned at the bookstore, which was absolutely nothing. Even more discouraging, what if Lou had taken my money and told me that the customer in my photo liked to look at wet shots in the privacy of his own home, or at pictures of Oriental transvestites? When you came right down to it, so what?

When I surfaced from the Harvard Square T-stop, the weather was no more threatening, and no less. The storm seemed likely to hold off till the evening. From the pay phone in the Tasty, I called the direct number Kellicott had given me.

"Tom Bethany," I said when he answered. "Any chance of seeing you for a half hour or so this afternoon?"

"Pretty tough, today. Is it something we could do over the phone?"

"Well, I need to know about a couple or three things maybe we shouldn't talk about over the phone."

"All right. Listen, I'll be tied up for probably another half hour," he said when I asked if I could see him again. "Can we make it for then?"

I said we could, and ordered some coffee. The Red Sox were on the radio. When the action in wrestling reaches the level of baseball's most exciting moments, the ref calls you for stalling. So instead of listening to the game, I got to thinking about something equally motionless, my background investigation of Kellicott. Gossip from the old headmaster and the young civil rights lawyer were the high points so far, but as Karl Marx said about John Stuart Mill, they drew their eminence from the general flatness of the terrain. The dozen or so other people I had talked to had nothing but praise for Kellicott. He was brilliant, patriotic, a devoted husband and father, a tireless public servant, a scholar of world renown, a generous, kindly, sensitive, thoughtful, and so on and so forth human being. But when the vote gets unanimous or close to it, I can't help remembering that the Tonkin Gulf resolution passed the Senate 88 to 2. And the only senators who managed to get it right were the two, Morse and Gruening.

They lost, though, and it looked like I would, too. I still had a credit check to run, and Kellicott's home life to look into. But if those wells turned out to be dry, as it seemed likely that they would, candidate Markham could announce his selection of Kellicott to be secretary of state. Still, like Morse, I would give it my best shot. After a second cup of coffee, I headed down JFK Street to the JFK School, which is just this side of JFK Park. All are located in JFK's old congressional district, which was now represented by JFK's nephew.

The windows to Kellicott's office were open, and he had the big floor fan trained on him. The clutter on his desk was weighted down with staplers, books, coffee cups, whatever was handy and heavy. Papers fluttered in the hot wind. Kellicott waved me to a chair and hauled the fan around so that it blew in my direction. Then he left his desk and took a seat beside me, in the breeze.

"How's it coming along?" he said. "Everybody cooperating with you?"

"Oh, yes," I said, leaving fat Lou and his punch-drunk swamper out of it.

"Good. I was afraid that various misguided souls might think they were doing me a favor by not talking with you." I noticed that he was calling me nothing—not Tom, or Bethany, or Mr. Bethany. He must have filed away my failure to pick up on his earlier invitation to call him Alden, and decided reciprocity was the polite and tactful course of action.

"No, pretty near everybody thinks you're great stuff, and they didn't mind telling me about it."

"Well, they probably want jobs."

I smiled. Whenever I saw Kellicott in person I felt less

hostile toward him. Like lawyers. In the abstract I hate them, but I like most of the ones I know. One of them I even love. And for most people, to know Kellicott seemed to be to love him. The only exceptions were his old headmaster and his old gofer at the State Department. If his gofer didn't like him, I wondered what his various secretaries through the years had thought of him; but my Labor Day deadline probably wouldn't leave me enough time to find out. First things first.

"One or two things," I said. "Do you have somebody to handle your business affairs or do you do it yourself?"

"Fellow named Harvey Atkins, at Atkins Sherrold Fitch & Bursley. I'll tell him you're coming. The main thing you'll find out is that I've got more money than any one person deserves to have. I made it the old-fashioned way, too. Married it."

Again I smiled back at him. "Any potential trouble with your investment portfolio?" I asked.

"Take a look, but there shouldn't be. When I first went down to Washington, I had Harvey clean it out, much against his better judgment. Sold Nestlé because of the baby formula flap. Sold all my stuff from companies that did business in South Africa. Don't eat grapes, don't drink Coors. Well, I don't go quite that far, although it's true I don't drink Coors. But that's because it's watery."

"What about your real estate? Deeds clean?"

"By clean I imagine you mean restrictive covenants. Actually, there was one on our property out on the Vineyard. Unenforceable, of course, but I wouldn't buy the place till they took it off. Which they did. Harvey can show you the papers."

"Ever had electroshock therapy?"

"Nope."

"Been to a psychiatrist or psychologist or anything at all along those lines?"

"Nope." Kellicott paused. "But maybe you should know that my wife had a pretty rough time psychologically when she was younger. I could put you in touch with her various doctors if you think it's necessary."

"Not unless it's still a problem."

"No, it's all behind her, thank God. Just an unusually stormy passage through adolescence."

"Ever been prescribed any medication for depression, insomnia, hyperactivity, or any other emotional or behavioral disorder? You, I mean, not her."

"Not insomnia, really. I've taken sleeping pills now and then, to help beat jet lag problems. I take Valium as a muscle relaxant when my back goes out, which happens once or twice a year."

"Do you take any other drugs at all?"

"Actually I don't. Except for the damned back, my health is perfect."

"Benzedrine, amphetamines, diet pills, Quaaludes, cocaine, marijuana, heroin, any drug at all that you can't buy over the counter?"

"Alcohol, but you can buy that over the counter."

"How much alcohol?"

"Sometimes I take a drink before dinner. Most times, I guess, although it isn't quite a daily habit. Wine is. We always have wine with dinner."

"Do you ever have severe hangovers?"

"Once in college."

"Any disciplinary action taken against you in college or graduate school?"

"Nope."

"Plagiarism, cheating?"

"Like poor old Joe Biden? No. Wait a minute, I take that back. When I was nine or ten I copied a paper from my best friend. My future brother-in-law, in fact."

"I imagine the Senate would let that one slide."

"I imagine so, yes."

"Anything in your past that might disturb a red-blooded he-man like Lee Atwater?"

"Am I homosexual, do you mean?"

"I have to ask."

"I know. The answer is no. Not even a schoolboy experience."

"What about rampant heterosexuality, then?"

"Like poor old Gary? No, I'm pretty well settled in at home. Actually, though, maybe there is something along those lines you ought to know about."

"What's that?"

"There was a time when I used to make the rounds of pretty nearly every strip joint and topless bar in the Boston area. I wouldn't imagine anybody would know that, but it would certainly look odd if it ever came out."

"What did you do it for, then?"

"My daughter Emily, who died. Didn't you say on the phone you were interested in her? Or was it my other daughter, Phyllis?"

"Both, I imagine. Emily at the moment, I guess. She was why you were making the rounds, you say?"

"Yes, she was why. I'd go out nights looking for her, try to get her to come home whenever I found her. Those are the kinds of places I had to look."

"Would she be a customer or working?"

"Working. Waitressing at first. Then on to the other things. Finally, of course, she got herself killed."

"You think that's what she was trying to do all along?"

"I sometimes think so, but who can say?"

"I guess you should tell me about her."

"All right, if you think it's necessary." Kellicott was still for a long moment, composing himself perhaps, or getting his thoughts together.

"Emily was a difficult child," he started out. "Right from the start, right from kindergarten, she had trouble with authority. She was so smart that school bored her. Well, it bored me, too, till I got to the postgraduate level. But I used school in a rational way. I didn't fight back against it the way she did.

"The first time she ran away she was only seven. She walked two miles to a school friend's house and asked to stay there. The friend's parents called us, naturally. Wasn't the last time we'd get calls like that, I'm afraid to say. By the time she was in the eighth grade, she had started to cut school and hang out at the malls. Sometimes she'd stay out all night, too, God knows where. When she was fourteen, she had an abortion ... This isn't too easy to talk about ...."

That was plain from his voice. I didn't offer him any encouragement; he'd have to decide for himself if he wanted to go on. He did.

". . . Do you know Buckingham, Browne and Nichols? They start them out in kindergarten, you know. Right up to college. All through the elementary years, she at least did well in her schoolwork, but then it changed. Drugs, I'm sure, even though the school never actually caught her. The worst boys she could find. The only reason she got into a decent college was because I got after her at the beginning of her junior year about her grades. Not that getting after her had ever worked before, but that year she took a few minutes off to get straight A's. I presume the idea was to show her contempt for the whole process, probably for me, too, by demonstrating how easy it was. It was enough to get her into Wellesley, though, just barely. That and the fact that she was a development case."

"What's that?" I asked.

"That's the delicate way that deans of admission refer

71

to a kid whose parents are in a position to build the place a new gym. Not that we ever got around to building one, or would have. Anyway, Emily managed to stick it out for a while without going to hardly any classes, but then she dropped out entirely in May of her freshman year. From then on she just drifted further and further away from us, just sank down and down . . ."

"Did she keep in touch?"

"Not directly, but I think she wanted us to know roughly what she was up to. She'd tell friends, and they'd tell us. Never exactly where she was, but in general what she was up to. And I'd go looking. Pretty tough stuff, to be sitting there in the dark in some sleazy dump, and see your daughter come out on the runway and take it off for a bunch of drunken sailors."

"Would you go backstage afterward?"

"If I could. Or wait for her outside. She'd laugh at me if she was sober, or scream at me if she was drunk or on drugs, or whatever she did. I never told her mother when I found her, or even that I was looking for her."

"Did she use her own name?"

"I don't know, actually. If part of the idea was to humiliate me, us, she may have used the family name. And made it clear to everybody just what family it was. I just don't know. I don't even know where she was living all those years, or who she was with, or what name she used. Not sure I want to know."

"Well, did they announce her by her right name when she danced?"

"I never really saw her dance. I don't think I could have stood that. I left before she came on."

"Then I suppose there's at least a chance that none of her new pals knew her real name," I said. "In any event, as long as Markham's people know about the situation in advance, I can't imagine it causing any trouble if it does come up. Hell, even the Eagleton thing could have been contained if he had been honorable enough to tell McGovern about it beforehand."

"That was my thought at the time, too. Very poor behavior."

"Do you remember the names of the places Emily worked?"

"Do you really need . . . Well, if you do, you do."

Kellicott reeled off from memory the names and addresses of the topless bars and strip joints where he had run across his daughter, and I just nodded instead of writing them down. We were two teenagers showing off our grips.

"I'm going to need to talk to your wife and your other daughter, too," I said. "What time would work out?"

"Let's see. Today's Monday. Friday they're taking off for the Vineyard. I'm going with them and coming back Sunday night, but they're going to stay on through Labor Day. So we should do it this week. I'll let you know when I set it up. That number you gave me at the Tasty is still the only way to reach you?"

"The quickest way, yes."

On the way out of the JFK School I spotted an untended phone on a receptionist's desk. Dialing nine got me an outside line, and I called the Boston office of the ACLU. It was after five, but Toby Ingersoll was still there.

"This is the guy you were talking to earlier," I said. "I've just come from talking to our buddy."

"Hello, guy I was talking to earlier. Are you calling from a bugged phone?"

"I doubt it. It's a phone right outside his office. I figured maybe I was calling to a bugged phone, though. Meese said you were a lobby for criminals."

"Sometimes we are, I guess. What can I do for you?"

73

"The time you saw our guy in the Zone, was it day or night?"

"Night. Eleven, maybe."

"Are you sure he was coming out of the bookstore?"

"Pretty sure."

"I mean, could he have just been walking by? Maybe just stopped in front of it to tie his shoelace or peek in or something?"

"It's possible."

"You don't have any specific memory of him coming out of the door?"

"Not really, no."

"Was he carrying anything?"

"In a plain brown wrapper? I don't remember. Probably I didn't notice. I was about to come out of the theater when I spotted him. Tell you the truth, I turned around right away so he wouldn't see me. When I looked again, he was gone."

"So he was in the Zone, but you can't actually connect him with the bookstore."

"Except that he was in front of it, no. I should have made that clear."

As I hung up, the receptionist came back to her desk. "Sorry to steal your phone," I said, hoping I looked like a visiting dignitary. "There was a number I had to leave for Professor Kellicott."

The woman smiled, just as if this made perfect sense. As it would have made perfect sense for Kellicott to be wandering the Zone at night, searching for his daughter.

4

I ATE AN EARLY SUPPER MONDAY IN EMACK & BOLIO'S ICE cream parlor—an Oreo cookie cone. For dessert I had a French vanilla cone. Then I spent the evening in the reference room of Widener Library, putting my notes together in some sort of preliminary order for the report I'd probably have to submit to Markham's people.

Throughout the evening, a storm threatened but never hit. The air was heavy, waiting. Tuesday was like Monday, hazy, humid, hot. I spent it running down more loose ends in the library. None of them seemed to lead anywhere interesting. Toward the end of the afternoon, physically and mentally stale, I gave it up.

Outside the weather had changed. Thunder rumbled a long way off. The sky was beginning to darken, and the light had the strange, clear quality it gets just before all hell breaks loose. I hurried toward my car so I could go out to Fresh Pond and run around it. I like to run in storms, even electrical storms. G. Gordon Liddy used to climb on top of haystacks when he was a kid, to conquer his fear of lightning. Presumably nobody ever told him that fear of lightning is a mark of sanity. Personally, I try to believe that I run in storms not because of the lightning, but in spite of it. The proof is that when there's lightning around, I abandon my usual treeless route along the Charles. Instead I run around the reservoir out at Fresh Pond, where the trees make better lightning targets than I do. And I'm willing to run a certain reasonable risk for the pleasure of being sluiced cool after a steaming day. And, face it, for the sensation of facing down the Furies. Come right down to it, maybe I'm as crazy as Liddy.

The weird, greenish light held till I got to Ellery Street, where my car was parked, and most of the way out to Fresh Pond. Then fat drops of rain began to splat on the windshield, making craters in the dust that covered it. In less than a minute water was sheeting down the glass faster than the wipers could throw it aside. The cars on Memorial Drive slowed down, headlights went on, traffic poked along at twenty-five or thirty, each car sending out plumes of water to both sides.

When I pulled off the road into the small public parking lot provided by the Cambridge Water Board, the rain was still driving and the wind was threshing the trees. Inside the car it was steamy and stifling. My clothes came off reluctantly, sticking to my sweaty skin. To run naked would have been best; a poor second best were the nylon shorts and Nike training flats I put on before getting out of the car.

I am alive by accident.

The first of my prerun stretches is a squat and I was just dropping into it at the last second that would have saved me. An instant earlier and the man running unheard at me in the storm would have killed me standing; an instant later and he would have had time to adjust his strike downward.

As it was, something made me aware of a presence behind me. I hesitate to get mystical about these things, but a good many years spent dealing with fast-moving, hostile opponents either develops more than five senses or sharpens the way the five work. A pressure in the air, a scent? In any event, I turned my head and caught movement on the periphery, and I spun right as I dropped. I swung my right foot like a scythe into his ankle so that his momentum pitched him forward. He somersaulted and came up to face me, a pale shape in the storm with the glitter of a knife in its hand.

To do his job he had to come in on me, but to do mine, all I had to do was wait until he came into reach. When he did, stabbing down with his right hand, I caught his wrist and pulled his arm across my chest. There was no calculation in this, just an automatic continuation of the hundreds of hours I had spent back in Iowa working on the Russian two-on-one till it took no more thought than breathing. With my left hand I took him under the right arm, crossed in front of him, and tossed him over my hip to the ground.

Causing pain is at the heart of wrestling as a sport. Pain is a tool you use to move your opponent the way you want him to move. He does it because the pain is talking to him, and what it is telling him is that his body is about to be torn or broken if he doesn't move to relieve the pressure. But the referee is there to keep you from breaking his body, when wrestling is a sport. Now it was no sport. Now I put my left knee into his back and deliberately popped his right arm out of the shoulder socket. He grunted and dropped the knife.

I held onto the dislocated arm while I made sure he

had no more weapons on him, and then let him loose.
When he turned to run, I got him by his trailing ankle
and brought him down heavily before he could take the
second step. He couldn't break the fall with his useless
arm, and so he came down with his full weight on that
shoulder. This time he screamed with the pain, but just
once, and then he lay there defiant. His lips were open
in a grimace of pain, but his teeth were clamped shut.
They were square, yellow, horselike teeth. He looked
Hispanic, with a trace of Indian in his features. I dropped
down to my knees beside him.

"Who sent you?" I asked. He said nothing.

"What's your name?" Still nothing.

"*¿Como se llama?*"

This time he spoke. "*Chinga tu madre,*" he said.
Between us we had now exhausted most of the Spanish
I knew.

I looked for the knife he had dropped, but it was lost
in the mud somewhere. I had another one, though, the
balisong knife I had taken off the black pug earlier. In
all my life I had never taken a knife from anyone, and
now, in a single day, I had done it to two men. I went
to the car and took the pug's knife from the glove com-
partment where I had tossed it.

"Come on, Pedro," I said, gesturing for him to get up.
"We're going into the woods where we can talk without
bothering anybody."

He didn't get up, and so I took him by the bad arm
and he followed it the way a bull follows his nose ring.
All that held his arm to the rest of him was skin, nerves,
blood vessels, and the complicated system of muscles
that previously rotated the arm in its socket. At the very
least he would have to sleep on one side for the rest of
his life.

I led him off to the right of the parking lot, past a

jumble of cables, cast-iron pipe, broken hydrants, and other Water Board debris. Once we were into a little patch of woods, hidden from the jogging path and the highway, I had him stop. All fight was out of him now. The shock had passed off and the pain made his face gray under its natural olive. The rain plastered his long black hair flat to his forehead. The strands hung down below his cheekbones, and drops ran off them. I shook the blade out of the butterfly knife, and he began to chant what I took to be a prayer. I wondered how many murderous bastards had ended their lives with a prayer to the God who was about to burn them in eternal fire if their beliefs were correct. He prayed faster as I approached him with the knife.

I took hold of his light jacket and carefully, slowly, sliced the sleeve off. My idea was to have a look at his shoulder. Once he saw what I was doing, he stopped praying, from the tone of him, and started cursing. It took me a moment to figure out why he was all of a sudden mad instead of scared. Then I understood.

I had paid no attention to what he was wearing, except for registering in a general way that he looked like a prisoner escaped from some Latin American jail, dressed in third-world surplus fatigues. Looking closer, though, I saw that he was wearing an Ellesse cotton outfit—what they call running suits, although I've never seen one worn for running. It probably cost a couple weeks' wages for an honest man. On his feet were a pair of Nike Air Balance shoes with bright blue patches that made his toes seem to glow. My man was a sharp dresser, and that was why he had abandoned prayer for curses. He cared more for his "Miami Vice" threads than he did for his soul, or even his skin.

Noting his concern, I sliced his sodden Don Johnson outfit to ribbons and left him standing naked except for a pair of ridiculous purple bikini undies and a gold Rolex. I took the gold watch; somebody I liked might find a use for it someday. Nobody I liked would ever find a use for a purple bikini, though, and so I sliced that off his body, too. By now the rain was slowing, but it still came down hard enough so that water ran from the end of his penis as if he were pissing. Maybe he was. I would have been.

Dislocations look much more serious than they are. The knob on the end of the humerus, now out of its socket, made a lump the size of a jumbo egg on the front of his shoulder. The lump was a dark, angry red that would soon turn black. It is a common enough injury in wrestling, and I knew from people who had been there that the pain was terrible. I also knew that a lot of the pain would go away, almost from one second to the next, once the bone was reseated. And I was pretty sure I knew how to do that, since I had twice watched team doctors do it.

I tried to get all this across to the man, talking slowly and simply and using sign language in case his English was shaky. He didn't say whether he understood. He didn't say anything. But I figured he must know some English, if he was functioning enough in this country to get a job as a murderer. I made it as clear as I could that I would put his shoulder back together and make the pain go away if he answered my questions.

"Where's the car?" I said. "*¿Donde está automobile usted? Car?*" I held up his keys, which were the only things I had found in his pocket. "*¿Donde?*"

He had to have followed me out there in a car, and its registration might tell me who he was. But there were plenty of cars parked in walking distance, and the storm was lifting, and I didn't want to risk leaving my captive while I wandered around trying doors like a car thief. I had to get finished with him in a hurry, in fact, since joggers and dog walkers and motorists would come drifting back into the neighborhood as soon as the evening sun came out. Already the sky was getting lighter and steam was rising from the soaked ground. The thunder was far in the distance as the storm moved out to sea.

My catch said nothing. He wouldn't give his name, he wouldn't say who sent him, and he wouldn't tell me which car was his. He just stood there, furious, scared, stubborn, and naked. And in agony. I felt as sorry for him as he would have felt for me, after stabbing me to death. I herded him back to the car, where I opened the trunk and took what I needed from the jumble of tools, implements, and equipment in it. Back in the shelter of the woods, I twisted a length of wire around the wrist of his functioning arm, and tied it above his head to the limb of a maple tree. Probably the circulation to his hand would be cut off after a while. I thought about that and couldn't work up much concern. With the old pawnshop Polaroid I kept in the trunk, I took a picture of his face. It probably wouldn't do me much good, but without a photograph I'd stand no chance at all of ever finding out who the man was.

After taking a few steps back toward the car, I turned around to give him a last chance. I told him I'd let him loose and give him back his keys and kiss his boo-boo and make it well if he decided to talk. He talked.

"Tu madre," he said again, and so I threw his keys over the Cyclone link fence, into Fresh Pond.

It would still be hours till nightfall, and the sun after the storm was bright as I drove back down along the Charles. I parked on Plympton Street and set out on my delayed run. My plan out by Fresh Pond had been to do intervals, but now I set out at an easy, steady seven miles to the hour. The loop up to Arsenal Street Bridge and back was a few yards over five miles, which ought to take me five sevenths of sixty minutes, which I tried to figure out for a while but then gave up on. Easier to run it and see what my throwaway Casio said at the end.

The footing was a little soggy, but not too bad. The pace was enough below what I could do if I pushed myself so that I was able to think about something other than my lungs and legs as I went along the riverbank. It occurred to me, too late, that I should have left the man loose and left him his keys. Then I could have driven out of sight, sneaked back, and followed him to which-ever car was his. At least that way I would have had his registration number, and might even have been able to trail him home.

No question but that there was a certain lack of bril-liance in walking away from a man who had just tried to kill you, with nothing but a snapshot to find him by. Why had he tried, though? Think it out. Could it have anything to do with the unpleasantness at XXX ADULT BOOKS VIDEOS XXX? Unlikely on the face of it, but barely possible. The man could have followed me from the store easily enough, although it was hard to figure out why he would have done such a thing.

Or he could have nothing to do with the bookstore; could have had my car staked out for some entirely dif-ferent reason. This would probably mean he had tracked me home at some point, which was a very disturbing thought. It meant that he could find me again, and that I would have to move. On the other hand he could have picked me up at the Tasty, which wasn't so disturbing. Plenty of people knew that I was in and out of there every day. From there he could have followed me to the library and then to my car—in which case he wouldn't necessarily know where I lived.

Those were the only two answers I could see to the question of how, but they didn't get me anywhere with why. No random maniac follows you in a driving thunderstorm, tries to kill you, and then, through the pain of a dislocated arm, keeps his mouth shut except to tell you what to do with your mother. But I couldn't think of why anyone but a random maniac would want to murder me. Although lots of people had reason to dislike me, I didn't think I was unpopular to quite that extent. At least not with anybody who was out of jail at the moment. It had been a long time since I had worked on anything that even involved a murderer.

And then it came to me I was involved, even though at a considerable remove, in just such a business right now. Somebody, after all, had murdered Kellicott's daughter. For there to be any connection, though, whoever wanted me dead would have to be somebody who knew that I was stirring around in Kellicott's past life. That narrowed it down to Senator Markham, Phil Jeffers, Arthur Kleber, and anyone else in the campaign that they might have informed; to Kellicott and, presumably, his family; to the Miltons' gardener and the past and present headmasters of Indian Mountain School and the assistant headmaster and librarian of Hotchkiss School; to Hope and Toby Ingersoll and the fat man at the bookstore, if he knew who Kellicott was; to the dozen or more colleagues and associates of Kellicott's that I had interviewed; and to anybody that any of those people had happened to talk to since. It wasn't a crowd that would fill Shea Stadium, but it was big enough.

And it was even a little bit bigger, now that I thought about it. A few days back I had telephoned my only cop connection, Jackie Carr, to ask him to find out about whatever dealings the Cambridge Police Department might have had with Kellicott over the years. Jackie had left a message with Ralph at the Tasty for me to call him back, which I hadn't done yet. Right now he'd be off duty, but I'd probably be able to catch him at the VFW. Why he did his drinking at the VFW was because his lieutenant had warned him to go light on the booze, and nobody from the cops that might snitch on him hung out at the VFW. Why he drank at all, or one of the reasons, was so he could face up to going home to his responsibilities. Jackie had a lot of trouble with being a grown-up.

I found Jackie Carr playing darts with a couple of other gentlemen of our generation. Baby-boom vets hitting the wall at forty, down at the VFW hall. After his pals had beat him, he brought his beer over and joined me.

"Fucking darts, you imagine?" he said. "Not like the old days, huh?"

Well, he was right about that. In the old days we would have been sitting around the bar in the USAID compound in Vientiane after work, wondering whether to get our ashes hauled at Loulou's, the White Rose, or the Bamboo Forest. I had known Jackie for about three weeks back then, before he was rotated out of the air attaché's office in Laos. I was just beginning my tour with the army attaché's office. We hadn't been real buddies even for those three weeks, but you wouldn't have thought it when we ran into each other in Kendall Square more than a decade later. I had forgotten he was from Cambridge, if I ever knew it. He had just gotten married and joined the police department. I had just come to town to see if I could get a Harvard education without going to Harvard. Naturally we went off to have a few beers together, three or four for me and maybe twelve or fifteen for him. I took him home staggering drunk and his wife never forgave me. She figured I was a bad influence on her Jackie. I knew about that. I had a wife once, too, and back then I was a drunk like Jackie. My wife always blamed my friends, too.

"Not like the old days," I agreed.

"Remember the meat rack?" Jackie asked. I remembered. It was a bar in the Somboun Hotel that stayed open later than the other bars in town, so that all the hookers who hadn't connected yet came by to make one last stab at finding a customer for the night.

"Those were the days," Jackie said, ". . . my friend . . ."

"We thought they'd never end," I finished. And so we didn't. In our young lives, the war seemed to have been going on forever. But we had all come a long ways since then, and Jackie and I hadn't really been friends then anyway, and some son of a bitch had tried to kill me a few hours back. Back to business.

"How's it going, Jackie?" I asked. "Still busting heads?"

"Shit, it's all paper work. Might as well be a fuckin' clerk, tell you the fuckin' truth."

"How's Catherine and the kids?"

"Ah, she's okay. Busts my balls a lot. Sometimes I think I ought to walk away. You had the right idea, Tom, you know it?"

"I didn't walk away. She did."

"Whatever."

"I got your message from Ralphie. Have anything on my guy?"

"Professor whatisit? Kelly something?"

"Kellicott."

"Fuck kind of a name is that? Anyway, he filed his daughter as a runaway with Juvenile a couple of times, way the fuck back in the seventies. Both times she showed up back home after a few days. Last year some asshole sideswiped his car in Inman Square and split. Got him pretty good, sixteen hundred bucks' damage."

"That's it, huh?"

"That's it. Except for his daughter got wasted, you heard about that, I guess. But you wanted him, not her."

"No, I want her, too. You know anything about it?"

"Only that we never got the asshole."

"Can you get me a look at the file?"

"Maybe. I guess I could. Over lunch I could take it out, maybe, something like that."

"Tomorrow?"

"I could see. Call me, okay?"

We talked about Laos for a while and what a good time we had had there, mostly him talking. He was envious because he had only done six months in-country, whereas I did two years with the ARMA office and then three more with Air America after I got out of the army.

"It was like being rich, you know it?" Jackie said. "On a sergeant's pay, it was like being a fuckin' millionaire. Bo pin nyang, have yourself a good time, who gives a shit? You're rich. Here I get hassled at the fuckin' VFW, I get a few bucks behind on my tab."

"How much you running?"

"Hundred sixty, hundred seventy, like that."

"Shit, let my client take care of it. I'm on expenses."

"Oh, yeah? What are you working on?"

"Background check for employment." I put four fifties, folded, under my coaster and slid it over to him. "Buy us both a beer with this," I said. "It's a big outfit. If we don't take their money, somebody else will."

I didn't need to pay his tab, since he had already agreed to get me the file for the price of a free lunch. But I wanted to get him in the habit of taking money from me, in case I ever needed something tough. Besides, it wasn't my money.

By 8:30, Jackie was laying a solid foundation for a brand-new tab at the VFW and I had broken loose from him. Not knowing where else to start, I decided to show the Polaroid of my Hispanic attacker around in every bar, restaurant, and hotel where I was acquainted. Since this meant mostly in the Harvard Square area, I started there. The night manager of the Sheraton Commander had hired hundreds of Hispanics over the years, but not mine. The owner of the Greenhouse Coffee Shop didn't know him, and I had no better luck across the street at the Wursthaus. Moving right along, I found Chris Cat-chick behind the bar at the One Potato, Two Potato.

"What makes you think he's from Cambridge?" Chris said. He was an old friend and I had told him the whole story of the attack.

"Nothing except he was here and I'm here now and I've got to start some place."

"And when you think immigrant you think of the food service industry?"

"Actually I do, yeah. If a guy ran into the kitchen hollering, 'Green cards!' he'd shut down any restaurant in Cambridge."

"Actually you're probably right, but that's a lot of res-taurants. Why don't you just buy me a Sam Adams and take your picture down to the union hall tomorrow morning?"

"Why is it I suddenly feel like such an idiot? Bring me one, too."

By the time I had finished breakfast Wednesday morn-ing—which was a microwaved portion of the stew I make and freeze every Sunday—I had worked out a story to tell when I got to the Berkeley Street office of Local 26, Hotel Restaurant Institutional Employees & Bartenders Union. My story involved a former employee of my fictional restaurant who had left some valuable stuff in his locker, and so forth. It struck me as a pretty good story, but I never got a chance to find out if it would have worked. Instead, I got lucky.

On my way to catch the T into Boston I got to thinking about the empty lot I was passing, where Mass. Ave. and Harvard Street come together. Till not too long ago the lot had held a funky, beat-up, 1930s Gulf station with a blue cupola on top. But the building disappeared over Christmas vacation, when most of the local landmark lovers would be off work, out of town, or not paying attention. The station had been bulldozed flat by its greed-crazed landlord, Harvard University. Harvard figured a hotel on the property would make more money than an old Gulf station would, and the hell with whether the old station was a wonderful piece of period kitsch or not.

Also the hell with whether a hotel would overshadow, literally and architecturally, the historic church next door. The Old Cambridge Baptist Church was a large, awkward, but oddly attractive pile of black stones. It wasn't the kind of place you'd go to for that old-time religion, from a pastor in a powder blue double-knit polyester suit, hollering hellfire sermons against the pope and the perils of the big city. Macon, for instance, or Lubbock.

In the Baptist house are many mansions, apparently, because Old Cambridge Baptist catered to an entirely different crowd. Its parishioners drove old VW beetles, carried books and babies around in backpacks, and ate tasteless stuff like tofu instead of tasteless stuff like grits. They let their nave be used for union rallies. Their basement was a warren of offices that promoted various liberal causes. Among other things, Old Cambridge Baptist was a principal way station on the underground railroad that carried refugees from Central America to extralegal political asylum in this country.

With nothing much more in mind than that a lot of Hispanics must hang around the place, I found the basement entrance and went in. A cramped corridor led from one end of the church to the other, with tiny offices on both sides. On the doors were signs, often two or three to a door, for committees for this and that, mostly justice, freedom, liberty, equality, fair play, and equally subversive things. I picked the Committee for the Brotherhood of the Americas more or less at random. Inside I found two college-age girls stuffing envelopes, and a thin young man only a few years older. A sign on his desk said he was Jeff Lichtenberg.

The young man listened to me politely as I told him the story I had dreamed up in the hall. This maid working in my motel in New Hampshire, an illegal from one of those countries down in Central America, heard that her cousin had beat it out of the country before the secret police, and on and on. Anyway, his name was Ricardo Sanchez, and . . .

"Ricardo Sanchez is about as common a name down there as Bill Jones or Jim Smith or something," the young man said.

"That's what Rosita said. She figured a picture would help." I hoped it wouldn't occur to Lichtenberg to wonder how come Rosita would be carrying around a picture of her long-lost cousin wringing wet. At least I had cropped the photo at the neck, so the dislocated arm didn't show.

"That's Jose Soto," Lichtenberg said.

"You sure? She wrote down Sanchez."

"Sure I'm sure. We helped him out with clothes and a place to stay when he first came here from El Salvador. A long time ago, probably four or five years. He couldn't even speak English then."

"Can he now?"

"Oh, now he's practically fluent."

"My understanding, she said he just got here a little while back and can hardly speak at all. Maybe it's a bad picture?"

"It's him or his twin brother. I couldn't possibly be wrong. He's here two or three days a week, helping out the various committees. He's the most dependable volunteer worker we've got. Although I haven't seen him for a few days, come to think of it."

"Got to be the same guy, then," I said. "About five-eight, five-nine, maybe a hundred and sixty? Sharp dresser, kind of California style?"

"Jose? I think he's still wearing the same Salvation Army clothes we got him when he came. Looks like it anyway."

"Can't be the same guy. Rosita says every buck he gets, he puts it on his back."

"Well, we'll soon find out," Lichtenberg said. He dialed a number, spoke in Spanish to someone, and then put his hand over the phone. "Jose's asleep," he said. "He hurt his shoulder and they gave him some stuff at the hospital that makes him sleep." Lichtenberg turned his attention back to the phone, listened and talked a little, and then hung up. I could see we were no longer pals.

"Jose was viciously attacked in the street last night," he said. "He was seriously injured and the use of his shoulder and arm may be permanently impaired. Are you satisfied?"

I made a gesture with my own unimpaired shoulders,

meant to convey that I didn't know what the hell he was talking about. It failed.

"And Jose doesn't have any cousin Rosita, according to his cousin Juanita. I thought all the publicity we put out about the break-ins scared you guys off, but I guess I was wrong."

"What guys, what publicity?"

"Give me a break, Special Agent Whatever Your Name Is. You send people to burglarize the offices down here eight or nine times I think it's been, over the years. Nothing ever missing except stuff from the files. Now you cripple one of the finest human beings I've ever worked with. A decent, humble, gentle man. Let me tell you something, mister, that man you hurt was worth a hundred of J. Edgar Hoover's cossacks."

"Hoover's dead."

"His cossacks aren't." This was true enough, so I ceded him the point.

"I think you'd better leave," Lichtenberg said. "I have nothing more to tell you."

"Fair enough," I said, getting up. "But there's something I guess I ought to tell you. Your boy Jose tried to kill me with a knife late yesterday afternoon, for no reason I've been able to figure out. He pretended not to talk English, and he was wearing probably five, six hundred bucks' worth of casual clothes. If you want to find out who's FBI, you might start there."

"I don't believe you."

"I didn't think you would."

It was early yet, and nothing useful to do till lunch. I walked on down to the Square and checked at the Tasty for messages. Detective Carr, it turned out, was free for lunch today and had suggested that I meet him at 12:30 at the Singha House, 1105 Massachusetts Avenue, if that was convenient. That was the substance of the message at any rate, although not exactly its style. What the counterman actually said was, "You just missed that asshole Jackie Carr. He says tell you half past twelve at the new Thai joint next to where the old Food Shak burned down. Call him you can't make it. Tell me something, Tom, how come you're hanging out with a prick like that? Fuckin' lush, you know he puked in here one night? I shit you not. Right where you're sitting, practically. What'll you have?"

"I was thinking maybe a western omelette."

"Ten, twelve years you been coming in here, I never knew you to order a western."

"It was the puke made me think of it."

We settled on a cup of hot water with a generic tea bag in it, and a sliver of lemon on the side. After a while the water changed color, and I drank it. When it was gone I wandered out to the public tables outside Holyoke Center and tried to watch the passing show. But instead I kept picking away at the puzzle of Jose Soto, who was still out there somewhere. Whatever had made him want to kill me yesterday would probably make him want to try again, and this time he would take a personal interest in the project. I would probably be able to find him, now that I had his name. But then what was I supposed to do? Reason with him? He had been tough enough or loyal enough or scared enough to keep his mouth shut through the pain of a dislocated arm; he wouldn't be easy to reason with.

And who was he loyal to or scared of, or both? It seemed likely to me that he was an FBI plant in the sanctuary movement, but it didn't seem likely that the bureau had ordered him to kill me. The FBI was too cowardly an outfit to go in for murder; slander, character assassination, and malicious prosecution were more its style.

Besides, the FBI would have no reason—or way—to be aware of my existence. A Tom Bethany had existed on paper from birth until 1980. School records, army records, Air America employment records, GI bill, social security, income tax at a very modest level, pilot's license, marriage license, divorce papers, a few stories on the sports pages. But the only part of this that would have involved the FBI was an outdated full-field security investigation in connection with my job flying for Air America, which was a CIA proprietary.

And anyway that Tom Bethany had disappeared at the age of thirty-two, as far as any bureaucracy was concerned. He moved out of his Allston apartment, leaving no forwarding address. His credit cards, all paid up, were never used again. His driver's license expired. His car was sold and his auto insurance was canceled. His phone was disconnected. He stopped filing state and federal income tax returns.

What had happened was that we pulled out of the Olympic Games way back in 1980. If Reagan can blame all his problems on Jimmy Carter, so can I. Maybe it's even partly true. Certainly I was focused for the first time in my life back then, and certainly the Olympic boycott threw me badly out of focus.

After Southeast Asia—not because of the war, but after it—I went through a long black patch. I got married, I went up to Alaska as a bush pilot, I had a daughter, I got drunk for years, I got divorced and broke. Then one night I vomited all over a pool table, and I began to get better.

During those years I was a bully. I wasn't generally the biggest person in the bar, but I had my little trick. I could wrestle and they couldn't. I only had to play my trick a few times before even the prototype Alaskan males—bearded, 250-pound six-footers—came to understand that I could make them cry from pain. And I would, too, and did, and that made me a bully no matter how much bigger they were than me.

One night, in an Anchorage saloon full of drunks wearing six-hundred-dollar parkas and white Mickey Mouse thermal boots, I went up against one of these bearded bears. He knew some of the same tricks I did, as I learned the moment we touched. An untrained man grabs you; a trained wrestler lays his hands on you light as a priest so that he won't have to release the muscular tension before he can make his next move. The big man's next move was a pretty good one, nearly unsignaled, and it nearly got me.

But I was enough better than him so that after a couple of minutes in which it could have gone either way, I had him helpless on top of the pool table, lying on top of three or four balls that couldn't have felt good. But my muscles felt rubbery and weak and they had already begun to stop doing what I wanted them to do. And then I vomited, all over him and the table. Neither of us wanted to go on.

Next day, I hardly wanted to go on with anything at all. There was the hangover. I was humiliated from having puked in front of all the world like a stumble-drunk Eskimo. Worse, I had unarguable proof that I had turned soft and fat: a two-minute workout had taken my strength away. I might still make an impressive show for the ignorant, tying up nonwrestlers in a few explosive seconds. But any of a dozen wrestlers I had beaten in my high school days would no longer have any trouble with me. Furthermore, I had lost my wife and my daughter long since. And I had lost my last two jobs because of unreliability and sloppy flying.

My hangover disappeared the way hangovers do, unnoticed. At some point in the late afternoon it just occurred to me that the pain wasn't there any longer. The shaking was, though, and so was the desire to start in on the beer that filled two shelves of my refrigerator. But I didn't do it, then or for years after.

Instead I went back to the lower 48 and got myself into the University of Iowa with the help of the wrestling coach. I did well by him, although not so well by my professors. But I was graduated, just barely, with a degree in political science. And next year I made the Olympic wrestling team.

It had taken five years of daily discipline and self-punishment, never letting go, never slowing down or even coasting, always whipping the shrieking machinery past old breaking points, on toward new ones. Only one goal was left, five years spent winning the chance to try for it. And then Carter made a schoolboy gesture that dumped those five years down the toilet. It was January of 1980, caucus time, and I was already in Iowa. I went to work for Teddy Kennedy.

Two things made me useful. I could fly, and I didn't look like a bodyguard. In both capacities, I wound up spending a lot of time next to the candidate. Well before the end, it had become plain that Kennedy was in a perfect double bind that would keep him out of the White House forever: he couldn't get elected if he didn't tell the truth about Chappaquiddick, and he couldn't get elected if he did. Along the way, though, I learned a good deal more about politics than I had at the University of Iowa.

During the general election I worked for the Carter campaign, which was just as educational, but less fun. Most of the Kennedy people had really wanted their man to win; the Carter people didn't seem to care much one way or another, except as it affected their employment. For a while I couldn't figure it out, since neither candidate was terribly exciting up close. Then I thought of Mae West's advice on choosing between two evils: "Always pick the one you haven't tried yet."

After the old actor won, I followed two or three Democratic policy advisers back east, where they planned on hanging out at the JFK School of Government till the weather in Washington changed. My idea was that there might be something to be learned at Harvard, something that would make sense of all the things I had seen in Asia and in America. But I had no money left, and an academic record that wouldn't impress a graduate school admissions committee. And so I settled into a house in Allston, across the river from Cambridge, with a shifting population of graduate students. My idea was to steal an education, since I couldn't buy one.

I stayed alive with one odd job of research or another, many of them coming to me from my political friends. From the graduate students I learned how to live on practically no money, and how to get as much education as I wanted for no money at all. There's nothing much to this, actually. It's easy enough to get into the lectures and the library, and what else is there about a university that matters?

One day, doing a little research at the JFK School library, I came across a Department of Transportation manual that told motor vehicle enforcement officers how to spot phony credentials. What it amounted to, if you wanted to read it that way, was a manual on how to create a false identity. Telling myself it was just for fun, I followed the instructions. Before long a fully documented Tom Carpenter existed, and it seemed like a shame not to let him out for a little run. So I moved out of my communal house in Allston, and Tom Carpenter

rented a one-bedroom apartment in a converted residence on Ware Street in Cambridge. He had a brand-
new passport. He had a Social Security number, too,
although his account was empty. But he put the number
on his applications for a driver's license, car registration
and insurance, and various short-lived bank accounts.
This Carpenter paid his rent and his phone bill by postal
money order. He had no credit cards and had never
applied for credit, and therefore had no credit rating
that anybody could check. The tenants of the three other
apartments in his house knew only that he was some
vague sort of a consultant, and that he kept politely to
himself. Tom Carpenter had an active official existence—an ongoing file, so to speak—only with the Massachusetts Department of Motor Vehicles.

At the time I saw shedding my skin as a project to
pass the time, an amusing stunt to pull off. Maybe. But
maybe I had it in mind that the last time I was on the
government's list it got me drafted. Or maybe I was still
hiding from my dead father, who used to make it home
one way or another after closing time at a roadhouse
called the Round Tuit, and then beat the shit out of me.
He died, driving drunk, before I got big enough to beat
the shit out of him.

Or maybe I just didn't like my old skin that much, and
made a sensible decision to leave it behind in Allston.
Whatever. In any event, the thing worked. I felt a lot
better with a hidey-hole not many people knew about,
and a name that the computers had forgotten. I liked the
feeling so well that I even went to the trouble of building
myself a third identity: a fully documented Alan W.
Bowen was in one of my safe-deposit boxes, ready in
case of need.

Maybe the need had come, since Jose Soto had been
able to find me somehow. But even if the FBI had hired

him to murder me, the bureau only knew what it had on file. I couldn't think of any way to locate the present Tom Bethany from the traces left in old files by the old Tom Bethany. Unless you knew me personally, that Bethany was long missing and presumed dead. And therefore nobody from his former life, in Southeast Asia, Alaska, elsewhere, was likely to have been behind yesterday's attack.

That limited it some, if not much. The new Tom Bethany had been hanging around Cambridge fairly visibly for a long time. Even if his address was a box number in the Brattle Street post office and his place of business was the terrace in front of Holyoke Center and his phone was the pay phone in the Tasty, anyone who cared enough could track me down eventually. But why would anyone care?

I crossed the street to the sidewalk phone kiosks, skirting a loose circle of Harvard Square freaks. They were kicking a ball back and forth, trying to keep it from touching the ground. I dialed Kellicott's private number. He answered on the first ring, and I put my question to him.

"Jose Soto?" he repeated. "No, I don't know him. Who is he?"

"I think he's probably an FBI informant," I said. "More to the point, he tried to kill me with a knife yesterday afternoon."

"Kill you! What for?"

"I don't know. We had a talk after I dislocated his arm, but he wouldn't tell me."

"Shouldn't you go to the FBI, if you think he's connected with them?"

"Eventually I may have to, but I'll stay away from them as long as I can."

"Well, you know your own business, but I shouldn't

think it would be very pleasant to know somebody is out there who wants to kill you. Or did you have him locked up?"

"No, I let him go. I try to stay away from the police, too. First I'll try to work it out for myself, who sent him."

"Well, I hope you do, and I'm sorry I can't help you. Oh, by the way, while I've got you, would Friday night be convenient to come by and meet my wife and Phyllis? Phyllis being my daughter."

"Friday's fine."

"About seven, then. Do you know where it is?"

"Actually, I do. I drove by on Sunday to have a look."

"Did you really? You're very thorough."

He sounded impressed, not offended. For a minute we talked about how hot it was, which everybody tended to talk about that August, and then I went back to my table. The sun would get up over Holyoke Center before long and make the terrace untenable, but for the moment it was all right. I opened my soft leather briefcase and took out one of Professor Davis's books on slavery. At the moment I was interested in the influence of Christianity on abolition. My unreached aim for the past fifteen years or so has been to find out why the people who govern the world generally act like idiots whether they are or not. Right now I was collecting exceptions to the rule, like the abolition of slavery. After all, here and there society got it right now and then. I thought these aberrations might help me understand the larger question, in the same way that madness helps us define sanity.

Everybody needs a hobby.

5

THE THAI WAITRESSES IN THE SINGHA HOUSE OPENED THE sewer gates of memory for Detective Jackie Carr. "The guys you had to get in with were the TCNs," he said, meaning the Third Country Nationals who worked for the embassy in Laos. "We had this Filipino guy over at AIRA, Tony Maldonado. Janome by any chance?"

"Nah, I never noom."

"Anyways, one night he takes a bunch of us to this place they called it the Turkey Farm, know why they called it the Turkey Farm? Account of all the girls gobbled. So anyways, they come out with this girl she was probly fourteen . . ."

"Jesus, Jackie, fourteen?"

"Hey, I know what you're thinking. No problem, though. She had the body of an eight-year-old . . . Anyways, the point I'm making here is after we come back, the cunt and me, Maldonado says . . ."

I left Jackie at the table, working on his fourth Amarit beer at $3.50 a pop. A few doors up was a copy shop, where the kid behind the counter agreed to do my job while I waited. "Police stuff?" he said, when he spotted the departmental heading on the Emily Kellicott homicide file.

"Naturally," I said, hoping I looked like Captain Furillo. I kept an eye on him while he ran the pages through, so that he wouldn't stop to read them.

Back at the restaurant, Jackie had had a chance to think things over and get cranky. "I don't know how hot an idea it is, you having copies," he said.

"Jackie, come on," I said. "How often do we get together, shoot the shit, huh? How was I even supposed to eat, if I'm reading all this shit at the table?"

"I could get my ass in a crack, is all."

"Nobody sees the file but me, Jackie. My word."

Just then the check came, and he forgot all about his problems in the pleasure of watching me fork over three twenties to the waitress. Once he had driven off to fight crime, I walked over to the Harvard faculty club. It was too late for a free cup of the coffee they set out at lunchtime in the reading room, but on the other hand the place was generally deserted after the waiters cleared the coffee things away. And nobody bothered you if you looked like you belonged. And the air-conditioning sort of worked. I sat down on one of the tufted leather sofas in the paneled reading room, to work my way through the thick police file. It began like this:

"Car 23 responded to report of a possible dead body 0634 hours 13 March 1986, Lowell Mall. Officers Flannery and Tedesco discovered apparent female hand visible in snowbank which witness showed them. Witness identified as Bobby Schmertz DOB unknown as he is a WM retard who is employed as a night watchman by the mall owners. Call to police was made by Schmertz who discovered alleged body. Scene of incident was secured by Officers Flannery and Tedesco pending arrival of undersigned. Arrival was effectuated at approximately 0720 hours accompanied by Medical Examiner A. M. Karpegis and Crime Lab technicians G. L. Williams and O. W. Moskow and photographer L. L. Lumpkin. Deceased was determined to be Emily Milton Kellicot, DOB 14 Jan 1960, of 37 Standish Lane, Cambridge, daughter of J. A. Kellicot also of that address. Victim was employed at Personal Leisure World in Lowell Mall. Cause of death determined by Medical Examiner Karpegis was strangulation and time of death was estimated at 48 to 60 hours previously (see attached coroner's report). Knife lacerations of the letters 'P' and 'L' were noted on the victim's breasts as well as semen in her vagina . . ."

It went on and on, for pages of tortured sentences, typos, crossed-out words, and misspellings. In this respect it was probably no different from most literary efforts by most lower-middle-level bureaucrats in any American bureaucracy, corporate or public. The only difference was that detectives weren't lucky enough to have secretaries to clean up their prose. My objections weren't stylistic, but substantive. Sergeant Harrigan just hadn't collected enough information, or the right information, or both. Nearly every sentence of the report raised questions that needed answers. I had hoped to be able to limit my contacts with the Cambridge Police Department to Jackie Carr, who already knew I was around. But that wouldn't be possible. I went to the pay phone off the faculty club lobby, dialed campaign headquarters, and got Phil Jeffers on the line after only a few minutes.

"You got anything?" he said.

"A lot of little things that haven't come together yet," I said. "Maybe they never will."

"Good."

"I need you for something, nothing much. I've got to talk to a guy named Sergeant Ray Harrigan, a Cambridge detective."

"What about?"

"He investigated the murder of Kellicott's daughter. I need to look at the paper work on it and talk to him. Can you have somebody tell him I'm coming?"

"Is this important? I mean, I'm not asking because it's hard. It's not. It's easy. I'm asking because it doesn't sound important."

"I know it doesn't, but I think it is."

"All right, I'll make a call or two. Get right back."

"Literally right back?"

"Should be." So I gave him the number of the pay phone, sat down nearby, and started to make notes to myself in the margins of the report that Harrigan, when and if I talked to him, wouldn't know I had already read. Phil Jeffers called back, sure enough, in less than ten minutes.

"Your guy, Harrigan," he said. "He knows you're on your way."

"Doesn't know why I'm looking into Kellicott, does he?"

"Come on, Bethany."

"Just checking. Who talked to him?"

"Nobody talks to sergeants. Baby Joe's AA talked to the chief." This meant the administrative assistant to Joseph P. Kennedy II, boy congressman from the Eighth District.

"That should work."

"Listen, how are you coming, Bethany? Number one,

your meter's running, and number two, we've got to get this thing on the track or off it by Labor Day."

"Shouldn't be long. Maybe another week. I'm going to meet the family for dinner Friday."

"Meet the family? What are you, marrying the guy?"

"Markham's the one that wants to marry him."

Sergeant Ray Harrigan's office in the Cambridge detective bureau was a cubicle with chest-high walls made of painted plywood topped with glass. On his desk he had one of those aluminum and Formica nameplates you can get made for you in the stores surrounding any military base. It read, "Lance Cpl. Ray Harrigan, USMC." A U.S. flag was to the left of his name, and a Marine Corps seal to the right. The display impressed me neither with his patriotism nor his toughness. Your typical Marine is a perennial adolescent with something to prove and very little to prove it with. The former lance corporal gestured me in when I knocked, and came out from behind his desk to shake my hand.

"Real good to meet you, Mr. Bethany," he said, with a hearty deference that seemed to me appropriate for an ex-jarhead in the presence of an ex–army grunt. Probably those weren't his sentiments, though. Probably he just figured I outranked him, since his boss had told him to see me. Marines are taught to grovel in a manly way before rank.

"Good to meet *you!*" I said, exaggerating the heartiness a little to see if he would notice. He didn't. He was about as sensitive to sarcasm as an Apple IIg. "Understand you're the man to see about the Kellicott girl."

"Sure am, Mr. Bethany. I've got the file for you right here. Why don't you just take a seat right here, and take your time looking it over? I'll just step out for a cup of coffee so I won't be in your way."

And so there I was, trapped into a second reading of the Kellicott file. Actually it worked out fine, because I thought of another couple of questions in the half hour before Harrigan came back.

"So what do you think?" the sergeant said.

"It's interesting," I said. "I never saw a police report before."

"Oh, yeah? I don't know why, but I had the idea you did security work for the campaign."

"No, nothing like that. I'm kind of on the personnel side."

He wrestled with that for a few seconds and then gave it up as none of his business. "Anyway," he said, "what can I do you for?"

"What this is all about," I said, "is this girl's father. He volunteered to do some stuff for the campaign. What do you think? Is there any potential embarrassment for the senator in this girl's murder?"

"I tell you the truth, I don't see how. I mean, it's already been in the papers already, you know?"

"Not where she worked," I said. "That wasn't in the papers."

"Well, yeah, that part . . ."

"Or the other places she worked, or this man Wales."

"Wales?"

"Lloyd Wales."

"Oh. Pink Lloyd, her pimp. Sure, all that stuff, we kept it out of the papers."

"How come?"

"I don't know. It came from high up. Higher than the chief, even."

"All that stuff could come out now, though," I said. "That's what happens in a campaign."

"Hey, what's the difference?" Harrigan said. "It's only his daughter, right? I mean, who gives a shit what the guy's daughter did and besides she's dead anyway, am I right?''

"Right," I said. "Only thing is, in politics you never know how the voters are going to react."

Harrigan thought over this bit of wisdom and found it good. "You got something there," he said. "What I was getting at, though, I don't know how long you been in the area, but back in the sixties, around in there, they had a case kind of like this, maybe you remember it?''

"A murder like this one?"

"No, it was this MDC captain, police captain, you know? He was cousin to a guy I knew actually. Anyway his daughter, the captain's daughter, she used to call herself the Plaster Caster, maybe you heard of her?''

"I guess I missed it. I was over in Asia for a lot of that time."

"Yeah, well, she was in all the papers with those plaster casts, and the point I'm making is everybody and his brother knew she was his daughter but it never hurt the captain none."

"Plaster casts of what?"

"Rock stars. She had a whole collection."

"Of rock stars?"

"Yeah, she'd make these plaster casts of their dicks."

There was a lot more I wanted to know about this, to tell the truth; during those years in Laos I had missed a good deal of American cultural history. But it didn't seem fair to the campaign to catch up now, so I hoisted our conversation back on the rails.

"Probably you're right it wouldn't make any difference," I said. "But you know how it is." I shrugged my shoulders to suggest that we were both in this together, doing the best we could to satisfy superiors who weren't as bright as they might be.

"We may as well get this over with, Sarge," I went

on. "Mostly your report looks pretty straightforward to me, but one or two points occurred to me as I was reading it . . ."

"Shoot."

"How did Emily get to work at this massage parlor?"

"Drove, I guess."

"Was there something in the report about a car? Did I miss it?"

"We didn't know about the car till after that report you got. The way we heard about it was a towing company pulled it away a few days later and nobody showed at the lot to pick it up. They ran the plates through the computer and somebody remembered the girl's name."

"When did they tow it off?"

"Couple days after the retard watchman found the girl, as I recall."

"How long did the towing company have it?"

"I don't exactly remember. Ten days, two weeks, in there."

"Anything show up in the car? Bloodstains, signs of a struggle?"

"I guess her father would have said."

"I don't follow you, Sarge. Her father?"

"He got the car, near as I can remember. From the company. I mean, she died intestate, so it was his car."

"Is there a chance she was killed in her own car, you think?"

"I wouldn't think, no."

"Where was she killed?"

"My guess would be she was killed in the guy's car."

"The murderer's?"

"Right. Pink Lloyd. Her pimp."

"It doesn't say he was the murderer."

"Official reports, you can't put down everything you know sometimes."

"You mean if you can't prove it?"

"Right."

"Was there any blood in Pink Lloyd's car?"

"She was strangled."

"She was cut, too, right?"

"Both tits, yeah. With Pink Lloyd's initials. 'P' on the left tit and 'L' on the right."

"The coroner's report said it was the other way around. 'P' on the right and 'L' on the left."

"They must've got it wrong. Let me see."

The sergeant puzzled over the report, moving his finger under the relevant words once he had located them on the page. His lips moved, too.

"I'll be goddamned," he said. "I could have sworn."

I had just wanted to see if he would get it, but he hadn't. And so we moved on.

"Maybe the coroner was looking at it from the girl's point of view," I said.

"Huh?"

"Probably what she'd think of as her left tit, we'd think of as her right tit. You see what I mean?"

Sergeant Harrigan frowned for a moment, and then his whole face lightened as the concept came clear. "Jeez," he said, "all the autopsy reports he's done, you wouldn't think he'd fuck up like that. Jeez."

"Well, there you go," I said. "Anyway, there would have been some blood from the cuts, right? That was why I was asking if there was any blood in Pink Lloyd's car. I mean, you know, if that's where he killed her."

"He would have washed it out, probably."

"Did you look?"

"You gotta understand we didn't come up with Pink Lloyd's name until maybe a week into the investigation."

"Plenty of time for him to get rid of evidence like that?"

"Right."

"The girl's clothes were under her in the snowbank . . ."

"Under her and kind of around. Here and there, you might say."

"But nothing missing?"

"No."

"Any cuts in her clothing?"

"No."

"Says here her clothes were bloodstained. A lot of blood?"

"I think there was a little on her hat. Not too much. The lab would have it on file."

"Why her hat?"

"Who knows?"

"So when she was cut she must have had her blouse and her bra and so forth, most of her clothes off. Otherwise they'd have blood on them."

"I would think."

"Why would she take her clothes off?"

"He was her pimp. He wanted to fuck her."

"Why not drive on home where it's warm?"

"He wanted to kill her, too."

"He wanted to fuck her *and* kill her?"

"I guess. That's what he did."

"Why?"

"Maybe she was holding out on him and he carved his initials on her so his other whores would stay in line. Niggers, who knows why they do anything?"

"What did he say when you asked him?"

"He said he was in Boston that night, and a couple of his whores said he was, too. Plus the bartenders in the place where he said he was."

"But he wasn't?"

"Shit, those people lie for each other all the time. You gotta understand, they're not like us. Give you an idea what kind of a liar this guy is, he swore up and down he was never even her pimp. Said he lived with her for a while the summer before but he never turned her out."

"That couldn't be true?"

"No way. You gotta know these people."

"He say anything else that isn't down here?"

"Not a fucking thing. I mean, not word one. We were talking along, you know, and I was getting to where I knew he did it, and so I read him his rights. That was it, far as him telling us anything. Fucking Supreme Court. Let me try to explain it to you how it works. We had him downstairs, all right? Just questioning him nice. So I read him his rights and he shuts up. Well, it just so happens at that point it turns out it's gonna be a pretty long time before he can get to a phone for a lawyer, you follow me? So a couple of us are trying really hard to convince him to talk to us, okay? Pink says nothing. Zilch. Not even fuck you, honkie motherfucker, like a lot of 'em say every time you ask them a question. Which only makes it worse for 'em, the dumb shits."

"Let me ask you something unrelated," I said, to cut short the seminar on advanced interrogation techniques. "All the people you talked to in the investigation, were any of them Spanish-speaking?"

"Maybe they could have spoke Spanish. To be honest with you, I wouldn't know."

"What I mean, did any of the hookers, bartenders, anybody that was involved at all, look or sound Puerto Rican, Mexican, Central American, that kind of thing?"

"No, none of them. That I would have remembered."

Next I had Sergeant Harrigan take me downstairs and introduce me to the chief lab technician. She turned out to be a tough, cheerful woman of around thirty named Gladys Williams. Probably you had to be tough and cheerful if you were a Gladys in a world of Jessicas and Tiffanys.

"Sure I remember the Kellicott homicide," she said. "Another feather in your cap, huh, Ray?"

"Get off my ass, will you, Gladys," he said. "Hadn't been for the Supreme Court, I would have closed that case two years ago. Fuckers Mirandized him right back on the streets."

"Sure, Ray."

"I don't want to take up any more of your time, Sergeant," I said, truthfully enough. "Can I call you if any more questions come up?"

"Absolutely, absolutely," he said. He seemed happy to leave; I got the impression that Gladys made him feel uneasy. She got out her files on Emily Kellicott as Harrigan left, babbling about how welcome I was to call him anytime, day or night.

"I think he likes you," Gladys said. "You must be important."

"No, I'm not."

"To Ray you are. The way Ray is, he's either at your throat or at your feet."

"You think he's wrong about the Kellicott case?"

"That the pimp did it? I don't know, maybe he did. But I've gotta tell you one thing. The way Harrigan works, he looks around until he comes across the first black, and then he stops looking."

"You were at the crime scene, weren't you? There was a G. L. Williams in Harrigan's report."

"That was me, yes."

"You remember it pretty clearly? Reason I ask is because Harrigan was shaky on a lot of stuff."

"I remember it like it was yesterday, as the man says. It was the first homicide I went out on."

"No fun if you're not used to bodies, I guess."

"Oh, I was used to bodies. Before this I was an assistant in the pathology lab at Mass General for three years. Bodies were my life, you might say. No, the thing was the girl herself. We had the same birthday, I saw from her driver's license. I was two years older, but still. There she was in a snowbank and there I was ... Well, you see what I mean. And she was gorgeous."

"She was?"

"You're going by the police photos, right? Forget that. Everybody looks like shit in those photos. Face it, they're dead."

"She looked pretty in her graduation photo, but nothing spectacular."

"You can't tell from photos, period. But if you've been around bodies enough, you can tell what they looked like alive. She had a dancer's build. Legs I'd kill for. Perfect muscle tone, she would have looked just as good in a bathing suit when she was fifty. Not a beautiful face exactly, but lively, you know?"

"You could tell all this from looking at a body in a snowbank?"

"I went to the autopsy. I told you, I took an interest."

"Tell me about the cuts."

"Right on her breast, here." She indicated the locations on her own breasts. "That was another thing. She wasn't anything like me otherwise, but her breasts looked just like mine. I mean, exactly. I've worked with cadavers a long time, but a thing like that still shakes you. You think, Jesus, that's *exactly* what *I'd* look like if some fruitcake carved on *me*."

"The cuts were pretty shallow, as I understand?"

"Right. Superficial."

"What I'm wondering here, it doesn't sound like some weirdo like Jack the Ripper, slashing her all to pieces."

"No. The idea seemed to be just to leave his mark."

"Or somebody's mark."

Gladys showed interest. "Speaking of ideas, you've got one, don't you?"

"Not yet. I just don't like Harrigan's. Tell me, is there any way of telling whether she was raped or she consented?"

"Not really. There were no marks or bruises on her body, apart from the cuts. Penetration occurred, because there was semen in her vagina. I combed her pubic area and recovered a few hairs that weren't hers. In case we ever catch anybody to match them up with. But none of that proves rape."

"Can you tell sex from the hair?" I asked.

"No. It's not even too useful for general coloring. Pubic hair is sometimes a different color from the hair on your head."

"You can tell race, though, can't you?"

"Oh, sure. From looking at a cross-section under the microscope. But it doesn't get you very far, knowing he was white."

"It wasn't in Harrigan's report that he was white."

"The son of a bitch left it out? Well, I'll be damned. Now you see what I mean about him and blacks?"

"Still, what does it prove?" I asked. "A white person, not even necessarily a man, right?"

"Well, you've got the semen, of course, but I see what you mean. The hairs could have come from a woman, a customer in the massage parlor, or anybody. They wouldn't have to be from the guy that killed her."

"What happens to that stuff?" I asked. "The hairs, I mean. Semen."

"In homicide cases I keep it till the case is closed, which could be forever. The semen specimens are in little plastic envelopes in the property room, locked in a refrigerator we've got in there. The hair is in little envelopes, too. Just tossed in with her clothes and all, all the stuff we took from the scene. In wire evidence baskets with the case numbers on them."

"Could I take a look?"

"Sure."

The property room was down the hall, guarded by a fat corporal who wouldn't let me in on Gladys's say-so. He had to call Sergeant Harrigan before he would unlock the grillwork door for us. Basket A128 held mostly clothing: a raspberry-colored down winter coat, a white wool beret, soft deerskin gloves the color of cordovan, panties with a Filene's label, zippered boots, a light gray wool skirt, and a beige blouse of some silky-feeling material. The clothes were dirty and discolored and crumpled, as if they had come from a ragbag.

"Neatness counts here in the property room, huh?" I said, trying to straighten the garments out enough to inspect them.

"Take a look at him," Gladys said, gesturing toward the front of the room, where the corporal sat oblivious, watching the soaps on a miniature TV. "He look like the kind of guy who folds things up? He's too busy leading the life of the mind."

On the beret I found a small, faint, brownish mark, shaped something like an arrowhead. Next to it a square had been cut from the fabric.

"There were two of those bloodstains," Gladys said. "I cut the best one out for my tests."

I couldn't find any other cuts or tears in the clothing. Nor did I see any other bloodstains.

"He must have cleaned his knife on her beret," Gladys said. "A small knife, from the marks. Apart from that, no blood anywhere."

"What do you figure from that?"

"I figure she had her clothes off, or there would have

been cuts in them. I also figure she was already dead when he marked her up."

"That part I don't follow."

"Because there was very little blood on her body, or in the snowbank. It struck me at the time."

"That's not in Harrigan's report."

"I didn't tell it to him because I can't prove it. It's only a guess, but it's a good guess."

"Things don't fit together very neatly here, do they, Gladys?"

"They don't, do they?"

I opened a small brown envelope, the type jewelers use for repaired watches, and tapped its contents out onto my palm. There were four pubic hairs, black or possibly dark brown. I tapped them back into their envelope.

"That narrows it down," I said. "A male or female Caucasian may have been intimate with her sometime in the . . . when?"

"Last few days before she died," Gladys said. "Or longer. Depends on how often she washed, how carefully. I mean, most days you don't have somebody like me come along, comb you out."

"And I suppose the hairs don't have to come from the same person the semen does?"

"Not necessarily, no. You might be able to tell with DNA testing, but we're not equipped for that."

"I get the feeling we're closing in on the son of a bitch, Gladys. What do you think?"

"Oh, yeah," she said, deadpan. "He's dogmeat now."

I opened the dead woman's large purse, but it was empty. Gladys fished another brown envelope, stuffed full, from under the rumpled clothes.

"This is the contents," she said.

"I know what's inside without looking," I said.

"What's that?"

"Used Kleenex all rolled up into little wads. Women just can't grasp the basic concept of the disposable tissue."

I emptied the envelope—and separated out the dozens of little Kleenex balls. The other contents were ballpoint pens, keys, various buttons fastened together with a safety pin, a pocket sewing kit, coins, MTA tokens, an emery board, a couple of restaurant toothpicks still wrapped in plastic, a checkbook, credit card receipts, a comb and a brush, an envelope full of discount coupons, a Chapstick, a dispenser for birth control pills, and four Life Savers twisted up in their wrapper.

"See what's missing?" Gladys Williams said. I shook my head. "I didn't notice it at first, either. No makeup. No perfume, no compact, no eyebrow pencil, none of that stuff."

"Is that unusual?" I asked, before I thought. Of course it was unusual, particularly for someone who worked in a massage parlor. And I found something else unusual when I emptied out a soft leather clutch, itself the size of a small purse. It held a small bound sketchbook, a half dozen needle-sharp pencils of varying lengths, a sharpener, and two kneaded erasers. The sketchbook was almost full with what seemed to have been visual notes to herself: details of a nose or an eye, fluid sketches of people in various poses and postures, the folds and wrinkles in clothing, quick lines suggesting how clasped fingers slotted into one another, or how glasses perched on a woman's hair. Many of the impressions seemed to have been of people on the subway; most of the rest must have been done at work.

"Are these any good?" I asked Gladys.

"I don't know. They look good to me."

They looked good to me, too. In a few lines that

looked easy but probably weren't, she had suggested movement, character, whole scenes. Often the movement was suggestive—the flinging and thrusting of pelvises and breasts. The faces I took to be the faces of topless dancers, B-girls, johns, emcees, whores. In one scene, four women were sitting in a sort of waiting room dressed in what looked like nurse's uniforms. Their attitudes suggested boredom; their expressions were a queer mixture of passivity and discontent. Presumably these were her colleagues at Personal Leisure World. There was turning out to be more to Emily Kellicott than had met Sergeant Harrigan's eye—or, as a matter of fact, her father's eye.

Her wallet held several credit cards, a driver's license, a Cool Cash card from the Coolidge Bank, and a student member card from the Museum of Fine Arts. The card had been two years out of date when she died. "Harvard" was on the line marked "School or College." Probably this meant she had taken courses at Harvard's extension school. I had done the same thing when I first came to town, before I had made my discovery that you didn't have to pay to take courses at Harvard. Not as long as you stuck to large lecture courses and didn't fool around with nonessentials like registration, grades, exams, and credits.

I put the dead woman's effects back into the big wire basket, somewhat more neatly than I had found them, and headed back to the police lab with Gladys Williams.

"What was she like?" I asked Gladys. "Judging from her stuff."

"Confident, self-assured," she said.

"Because she didn't use makeup?"

"That, and her clothes. She wore what she liked, not what the other women in that massage parlor must have worn. Good stuff, nothing fancy or showy. Functional.

And she was neat. I carry a hairbrush, too, but mine is all full of hairs. Hers was clean."

She reflected for a moment, and went on. "Probably kind of a go-to-hell person. I mean, think of her sitting in those dumps with a sketch pad. I've never been in topless bars or strip joints, but would most of the people there want you drawing pictures of them?"

"I doubt it."

"She had to be tough, then. And together. Look in my purse, it'd be full of trash, useless junk. Old ticket stubs, grocery lists, cash register slips, gum wrappers. She kept hers shaped up. Nothing much in there she didn't need, except the old MFA membership card."

"What about that?" I said. "Would you mind making a call or two for me? It'd have to be a woman's voice."

I explained what I was after, and she agreed to help. Gladys turned out to be an accomplished liar over the phone, and it only took her two phone calls to make sense of the expired museum pass. The first was to Harvard's extension school and the second to the Museum of Fine Arts. Then I made a third call—to the painter who had taught Emily Kellicott's advanced drawing workshop two years before her death. Gladys had gotten the name out of the course director of the museum's art school. By now it had been four years, but Gregory Emmett remembered Emily well.

"She didn't really need me," the painter said. "Emily was a first-rate draftsman already. In fact I hate to admit it, but she was better than me. Most of my own work is nonrepresentational, and my drawing has gotten pretty rusty. Emily had a wonderful line. You know Ellsworth Kelly's work?"

I didn't.

"Anyway, her line reminded me a lot of Kelly's. Very pure, very spare. I encouraged her to take life classes."

"Meaning nude models?"

"Right. There's nothing like it for building fluency."

"Well, from her sketchbook she took your advice."

"It was terrible what happened to her. I felt so bad when I read it in the paper. All that life. All that energy. All that determination."

"What kind of determination?"

"To make an artist of herself. Her portfolio must have been two inches thick at the end of the course. She'd just take the assignments as a place to start, and then go on from there. She must have spent most of her waking hours sketching."

"Do you happen to know what she did for a living?"

"Anything to make ends meet, I'd imagine. Like most art students. Come to think of it, I think she said she was a cocktail waitress."

Emily Kellicott was starting to look very different from the coked-up wreck that her father described, or the whore murdered by her pimp that Harrigan saw.

"Tell me something, Gladys," I said after I hung up. "I've met three members of your department. A detective named Jackie Carr, and Sergeant Harrigan, and Corporal Whatever, the property room guy over there. Would you say they were typical?"

"Put it this way, there's a lot like them. It's the bell curve."

"Bell curve?"

"Face it, half of the world is below average."

"Yeah, but there's different averages. There's your average lawyer, your average stockbroker . . ."

"I don't know how much difference that makes. For instance I've seen plenty of doctors and plenty of cops. Maybe the doctors are better educated, but I can't see that they're much smarter, on average."

I thought about this and it seemed probable, all right,

if a little depressing. The army was the only organization I had done much time in, and certainly officers, as a group, were no brighter than enlisted men. Nor did it seem to take much brains to make rank, as I told Gladys.

"Same way in the department," she said. "In fact, the smartest people are mostly pretty well down in the chain of command."

"Who's the highest smart guy in the chain of command?"

"Billy Curtin. Deputy chief of detectives."

"I may not need to talk to him. But if I ever do, will you introduce me?"

"Sure."

"Okay, fine. One more thing. Will you go out to dinner with me tonight?"

"Actually, no. You're too much better-looking than I am."

"Help me back on board here. What are you talking about?"

"Well, people that go out together ought to sort of balance, you know? For example, we're both smart, so that balances. But you're kind of low-incredible handsome and I'm kind of bottom-third-of-the-class plain except for my tits, so that puts us out of balance, see what I mean? Now if you were sweet but really stupid, for instance, or if I were really rich . . ."

"What about if I were just asking you out to dinner?"

"My experience, men don't just ask women out to dinner."

"I do. The thing is, Gladys, I'm sort of a one-woman dog. Only the woman is married to somebody else and lives some place else, so I don't see her much. Anyway, the long and the short of it is that I don't give a shit for most men and they don't seem too crazy about me either, so most of my friends are women. And they're just friends, and she knows all about them. In fact she's met most of them. They range in age from seventy-four to nineteen going on twenty."

"That's some of the weirdest shit I ever heard. You're kind of a heterosexual walker?"

"What's a walker?"

"It's like that guy that used to escort Nancy Reagan to openings and stuff, what was his name?"

"I never kept tabs. Tell you the truth, it was almost like I didn't care."

"Anyway, a walker is a gay guy that makes his living going out with rich ladies while their husbands are off stealing more money."

"That's me, a heterosexual walker. Want me to walk you to dinner?"

"I've got to be the one who pays, then. That's the way it works, with walkers."

6

I HAD DRIVEN PAST LOWELL MALL DOZENS OF TIMES WITH-
out particularly noticing it. Mall was much too grand a
name. It was one of those small, dingy, suburban shopping centers that had preceded the giant malls. Its
ground-floor tenants were a cut-rate drugstore, a liquor
store, an electronics store, a video rental, an ice-cream
parlor, a tanning salon, and a shop for the full-figured
woman. All the shops were still open when I drove up,
just before five, but there was no problem parking. The
pavement was cracked, and weeds grew wherever they
could put down roots. I parked next to a large dumpster
that smelled of garbage.

I looked around the lot, trying to imagine how it
would have looked on the night of Emily's death. Cars
going by regularly on the parkway, but their lights not
reaching far into the parking area. The shops would have
been closed at that hour. Two streetlights, one at either

end, but no way of knowing if they were both working. Piles of dirty snow here and there, where the plows had pushed them. And coming out of one of them, a hand.

At first I didn't spot Personal Leisure World. Its sign was on the second floor, which was the top floor of the low, adjoining buildings that made up the complex. The entrance at first seemed to be through the neighboring drugstore, but after I struck out there, I discovered an unmarked glass door nearby that opened on to an unmarked concrete stairway. At the top was a cheap door, the hollow-core kind made of veneered plywood so flimsy you could put your fist through it without much trouble. A Formica sign said PERSONAL LEISURE WORLD, SAUNA AND MASSAGE.

Nobody seemed to be home when I opened the door, but I heard the noise of a TV somewhere. In front of me was a shelf sticking out of the wall, with an open photo album on it. The pockets in the Plasticine pages held color Polaroid shots of women wearing bikinis. The four I could see were called Wendy and Terri and Toni and Donna. To my right, an opening in the hall at waist height seemed to lead to an inner office. I caught a flash of movement behind it, and then a woman wearing a terry cloth bathrobe and slippers came from around the corner.

"Oh, hello," she said. "I didn't hear you come in. Anybody special you wanted to see?" She was older than the women in the album, and was just starting to become matronly. Her voice was deep and pleasant.

"I saw you had saunas," I said. "How much for just a sauna?"

"Thirty dollars," she said.

"Thirty dollars," I repeated, in a tone that perhaps conveyed a certain sticker shock.

"But a massage is only fifty dollars," she said, "including use of the facilities."

"What are the facilities?"

"The sauna."

"All right," I said. "Fine." Actually, it wasn't particularly fine. I hadn't been to a massage parlor since leaving Southeast Asia, and hadn't really felt the urge, either. But the prospect of sticking the Markham campaign for a fifty-dollar massage was an attractive one. The woman showed me to a cubicle down the hall with a sink and a massage table in it. She gave me a towel and a little bar of hotel soap. "The showers and sauna are just around the corner," she said. "When you're ready, just ring this button right here. Toni will be your masseuse." I tried and failed to remember which one of the photos had been Toni's.

The sauna was clean and newer-looking than the rest of the place, and so I suspected it didn't get much use. But it wasn't a bad unit. No one seemed to be in charge of the operation, so I ducked out and scrounged around till I found an empty soda can in a wastebasket and a scrub brush in a broom closet. I filled the can with water to pour on the hot rocks, and sat down to wait till a good sweat broke. After three cold showers and nearly an hour, scrubbed raw with the brush, mottled pink from the heat, I had had enough. I went back to my cubicle, lay down on the massage table with the damp towel draped over my middle, and rang the buzzer. I nearly fell asleep in the few minutes it took Toni to arrive.

She was a young woman, maybe no more than twenty, who was at that awkward stage when baby fat hasn't quite turned to the solid, permanent, adult fat soon to come. We must have the only civilization in the history of the world where the poorer you are, the fatter you are. We ought to send our entire production of potato chips, Twinkies, and Coke to Ethiopia, and keep the whole grains and powdered milk here for the Tonis.

It didn't seem likely she would have been here for two years, but I asked anyway as she kneaded inexpertly at my shoulders. "You ever know a girl called Emily, used to work here?"

"I never knew anybody named Emily at all," she said. "Probably it was before my time. I only started here a couple months ago, actually."

"No, this was a couple years back."

"Couple years?" she said, as if I had brought up some impossibly remote historical period, like the reign of Queen Victoria or the Carter presidency. "I don't think any of the girls was around that long ago, except probably Wanda."

"Is Wanda around today?"

"Oh, sure. Wanda's the manager."

I shut up and tried to enjoy the massage, but failed. My massage standards had been established nearly twenty years before on Bangkok's Patpong Road, where the massage parlors are the size of hotels and the masseuses the size of Girl Scouts. They were generally light-hearted, laughing and giggling a lot as if there were something irresistibly comic about sex. As of course there is. But Toni didn't seem as if she knew how to laugh by herself, without a sound track to show her when to do it and how hard. The Thai girls would walk up and down your spine with bare feet, which you'd figure would cripple you but it never did. With Toni it would. She would go, I guessed, 165 or 170 pounds. And, for all her size, she had hands that were weak and hesitant instead of strong and sure.

When she had finished and I lay on my back, the

towel still keeping me decent, Toni said, "How about a special, honey?"

The words were charged with romance. I was reminded of the summer when I was fifteen and visiting relatives downstate. My older cousin took me to a whorehouse in Hudson, New York, where he paid for our two whores to put on a show before I lost my virginity. The only line I remember was when the naked woman doing the memorized voice-over sat on the other woman's lap. "This is the way the boss gives dictation," she said. "More dick than tation."

Instead of walking out, we both went ahead with the awful business. But now and then, here and there, we pick up a little sense as we grow older.

"Not today," I said to Toni.

"Regular special is only a twenty-buck tip, honey," she said. "Special special's whatever you feel like giving."

"What's a special special?" I asked.

She ran her tongue over her lips, the way models do in the TV ads that show lipsticks sliding out of gleaming plastic foreskins.

"Do you take dictation?" I asked.

"Huh?" she replied.

"Never mind about the specials," I said. "You can have the twenty, though. I hit the numbers yesterday."

"Oh, wow," she said, coming to life at last. "Every day I play and my girlfriend, like she never plays and last winter she hits for five hundred bucks. I'm like Debbie give me a break, okay?"

"Huh?" Wanda asked. I had spoken clearly enough, but she must have figured she misheard. It probably wasn't a request the manager got every day.

"A receipt. I'm on expenses."

Wanda got a block of forms out of her desk and leaned forward as she began to fill one in. This let her terry cloth robe gape open so that I could see her breasts, which were still good. The receipt forms were the standard ones you can buy in any stationery store. Probably she used them mostly for tradesmen delivering supplies. At the top, in a neat, parochial-school script, she wrote out "Personal Leisure World."

" 'Received by,' " she read off the form. "What name you want me to put?"

"Tom Bethany. B, E . . ."

"Oh, I know how to spell it. It's where Jesus stole a horse."

That was certainly the way a D.A. would have looked at the matter, although it isn't exactly the slant St. Luke gives to the story.

"Not too many people know that," I said.

"You didn't know that stuff cold, you got a whack with a steel ruler from Sister Margaret," Wanda said. "I see nuns on the street to this day, I feel like hiding my hands behind me."

Wanda wrote down my name, and looked up at me again. "Mostly, what I use these for, it's for janitor supplies or laundry or something. What do you want me to put on it that it's for?"

"Just say 'massage.' "

"Your boss not going to mind?"

"I don't have an actual boss. I'm kind of a consultant."

"Yeah, but still . . ." She was signing the form. Wanda Vollmer.

"Well, this is kind of what I'm consulting on."

"On massages?" Wanda said. She had torn the receipt off the pad, but now held on to it.

"I'm working with Emily Kellicott's family."

"What are you, insurance?"

127

"No."

"A lawyer? We're gonna get sued, that's it?"

"No."

"Well, what?"

I gave her a card identifying me as vice president for research of Infotek, Inc. She inspected it and said, "I don't get it."

"Well, the thing is, the Kellicotts were never happy with the police investigation. So they asked us to go over the same ground and make sure everything was done that could be done, you know?"

"You're a private investigator?"

"No, no. Tell you the truth, this is pretty much out of our line. Mostly we do library research, computer research, that kind of thing."

"I told everything I know to the police."

"I know you did. Sergeant Harrigan gave me a copy of the report."

To establish how official I was, I took the report out of my briefcase and let her look it over. Wanda skimmed a few pages. She gave it back, along with my receipt for the fifty dollars.

"Well, everything must be in here, then," she said. "I told that dumb son of a bitch . . ."

"Harrigan."

"Whatever. I told him everything I knew about it. Which was nothing."

"I know you did. But I was wondering about other stuff, about the girl herself. For instance, I was wondering about the pictures she drew."

"How'd you know about them?"

"She had some of them in her purse."

"They were something, you know it? She did 'em just like that." Wanda made rapid scribbling motions in the air. "They didn't exactly look like the person, not like a photo, but you could always tell who they were. I could never figure out how. A few lines, but you could always tell."

"She ever do customers?"

"Mostly the other girls. Maybe once in a while one of her regulars."

"Do most girls have regulars?"

"Well, you take a girl like Toni, she won't have no regulars to speak of. Nelda, though, regulars is practically all she had."

"Who's Nelda?"

"Nelda was like her stage name, I guess. I never knew it was really Emily, until the police said it."

"Okay if I sit down?" I asked, doing so. "How come was it that Nelda had so many regulars? Because she was so pretty?"

"Only partly. You got to understand what sort of person Nelda was. Normally girls that do this kind of work, to be honest with you they're not real bright. And mostly they're lazy. It's work for lazy people. Nelda was different."

"How was she different?"

"I don't even know where to start. She was always moving, always doing something, for one thing. And she dressed different, like a college girl. She never wore makeup, kept her fingernails short, hair short. She talked different. In fact, I was surprised to find out she was even from around here at all, the accent she had."

"She never mentioned about her family, then?"

"Never a word. I remember once one of the girls says something about Father's Day was coming up or something, you know, and Nelda goes, 'They got a day for those bastards now?' So dumb me, I ask her what's the matter, you don't get along with your dad? 'My father's dead,' she goes. 'He died when I was thirteen.' "

"Which wasn't so," I said.

"I saw in the papers, yeah. But she never said another word about her family."

"Why did she work here, Wanda? What's your idea?"

"I don't have to give you my idea. I asked her once and she told me. She was here for the drawing."

"So she could use the other girls for models?"

"Partly that. A lot of the time, like I said, there's not much to do and she'd get out her big pad. But mostly it was the hours. She came on at four and so she had most of the daylight hours to work outdoors. From what she told me, the light at various times of day is important."

"When do you close?"

"Ten, and that's another thing. You're talking money, I got no doubt she probably did better in the clubs. But with the clubs, you're not out of there till three, four in the morning, maybe five, and you wind up sleeping most of the day."

"What did she do in the clubs?"

"Topless. She did some stripping in a couple clubs in the Zone, too. You don't see too many bodies like hers down there, I'll tell you."

"Dancing, was it?"

"Did she turn tricks, you mean? I'd be amazed."

"What about here?"

"Nobody turns tricks here. Why? Did that dumb cow try to make a date with you?"

"Toni? No, she just wanted to sell me a regular special or a special special."

"Yeah, well that's not tricking. That's a handjob or a blowjob."

"Did Emily do specials? Nelda, I mean."

"Handjobs is all. Anybody'd ask her about blowjobs, she'd always tell him she was saving that for when she was married."

"They didn't mind?"

"No, she said it so's they'd laugh. I'll tell you the truth, most of them would have gone to Nelda even without the handjob."

"How come?"

"Just for the massage, would you believe it? She read a couple books about it and she used to know this girl that was Chinese or Vietnamese, some kind of Asian anyway, and she taught her a lot of stuff they do over there. Plus Nelda had a personality. Guys liked her. Some of them liked her a lot. She handled them just right, a friend but always professional, if you see what I mean."

"The ones who liked her a lot, did any of them come by the night she was killed?"

"Only Pink Lloyd."

"The pimp?"

"That's the only Pink Lloyd there is."

"To get money or what?"

"He wasn't her pimp."

"The police say he was."

"Well, he wasn't. I told that to that guy, that Harrigan. He wasn't ever her pimp."

"What was he, then?"

"He was an ex-boyfriend."

"Why would a pimp have a girlfriend?"

"You'd have to ask him."

"You ever ask her about it?"

"Not in so many words, no. But my impression was they were together for a while when she first worked in the clubs, and it pissed off his regular girls, the working girls. Whether it was that or what, I don't know, but from what I understand, recent years, she'd only see him now and then. Like she was sneaking around with a married man, you know?"

"I know, all right."

"My impression was it was okay with her that way. From stuff she'd say."

"What kind of stuff?"

"Once she said he was like custard cream pie à la mode. You might want to duck out for some now and then but you wouldn't want it as a steady diet. If that makes sense."

"I can see where it might," I said. "Tough if you're the pie, maybe."

"Personally I could see her point," Wanda went on. "But plenty of girls wouldn't mind Lloyd for a steady diet."

"What's the attraction?"

"Well, you know, people say 'pimp' like it's a dirty word. But there's pimps and pimps. I'd have to say Pink Lloyd isn't too bad a guy, as far as pimps go. Plus which, they tell me you can't look at him without wondering what it'd be like with him."

"They tell you? I thought you knew him."

"I do, but I'm not them."

"There's women like that, too," I said, thinking of Hope and the roomful of lawyers.

"And Nelda was one of them," Wanda said. "I guess you never knew her, huh?"

"I'm just starting to. Did the other girls resent her?"

"Why would they?"

"My experience is that if men really like a woman, she generally doesn't have many women friends."

Wanda considered this. "Generally, I guess that's right," she said at last. "But even if Nelda had a lot going for her, you couldn't feel jealous of her. She'd never take a man away from another girl. In fact she didn't even have any men that I knew of, except sometimes Pink Lloyd. You just kind of felt good around her, somehow. She dressed her own way, talked her own way. Never tried to hide that she was different. Better, really, and we all knew it. But you didn't feel like *she* knew it. She was what she was, that's all. Like it wasn't specially good or bad, but just what she was. I don't know, it's hard to put it into words."

"You're doing fine."

"Well, she was just real nice to be around, that's all. If she'd have had a real funeral, I bet everybody she ever worked with would have been there."

"What kind of funeral *did* she have?"

"Some kind of private service just with family and then they cremated her. She would have looked real pretty in makeup, too."

Wanda paused, as if seeing the funeral that might have been. With Nelda looking real pretty, in the makeup she never wore alive.

"I'd like to get my hands on the prick that killed her," she said. "The son of a bitch would be singing soprano."

"You sound like you'd really do it."

"Bet your ass I'd do it."

"What if it was Pink Lloyd?"

"It wasn't."

"The police think it was."

"The police don't know shit."

"His initials were carved on her."

"Not by him."

"Why not?"

"Look, I've had two different girls worked here, they went on to work for Lloyd. So I know how he does his business. Plenty of pimps, they beat up on their girls, but not him. A girl keeps getting out of line, all he does is he tells her to take off, don't come around no more. So the only ones that get out of line are the ones so fucked up you wouldn't want 'em around anyway.

Everybody else in the life knows what a good deal they got with Pink Lloyd. He takes care of 'em, treats 'em good, lets 'em keep a fair share.''

"That's how he treats his working girls, okay. But she wasn't one of his working girls.''

"I hear what you're saying. You mean if he loved her, who knows what the hell he might do? You're wrong, though.''

"Somebody carved his initials on her.''

"Not him.''

"How do you know?''

"Because she had her clothes off.''

"That's what I thought, too,'' I said. "Somebody you've known for years, why would you do it with him in the parking lot?''

"Particularly in the cold.''

"Right. So who, then?''

"The guy that walked out on her.''

"What guy was that?''

It turned out that a man had come into Personal Leisure World the night of Emily Kellicott's death. He wasn't a memorable man, at least not to Wanda. Nothing particular about him that remained in her recollection: she couldn't say if he was thin or fat, short or tall, young or old, handsome or homely. She couldn't remember the color of his hair or of his eyes; she couldn't recall how he was dressed or whether he was fair-skinned or dark, except that he was a white man. This ruled out the extremes—he wasn't Abbott and he wasn't Costello, for example. But it probably left hundreds of thousands of possibilities, just in the Boston area.

"Did he have an accent?'' I asked. "Mexican, South American, like that?''

"No, no accent. Nothing special about him.''

This nobody man had showed up sometime around eight or nine. That was the last Wanda saw of him.

"I was in and out of the office," Wanda said, "and I must have missed him when he left. Fact I didn't even know he was gone till Nelda come out and said the guy took off without his massage."

"Does that happen much?"

"Now and then a guy loses his nerve, changes his mind, whatever. It don't make shit to me, long as he doesn't want his money back."

"What if he does?"

"Fuck him," Wanda said. "Anyway, I wouldn't have paid any attention at all, except Nelda sounded funny when she told me the guy split. I asked her did he try anything weird or what, but she said no, it was nothing. And that was it. I wouldn't have ever thought of it again except for what happened."

"He's not in the police report, this guy. Did you tell Sergeant Harrigan about him?"

"I told him, but he said it didn't mean nothing. What did the cop care? He already had it figured out. Sure he did."

"What about Pink Lloyd? Did he show up before or after this guy?"

"After. The next customer, in fact, except he wasn't a customer. He just came to say hello or something, which was okay because she was between guys. So he did. Said hello."

"How long did he stay?"

"Maybe twenty minutes, maybe a little longer. Nobody else came in for a while, so she was free. They talked in the little kind of room we have for the girls in the back. I buzzed back when I finally needed her."

"Did he leave then?"

"Nelda came out with him and walked him downstairs. I guess he left."

"He could have hung around, though?"

"He could have."

Wanda and I talked for another ten minutes or so, until a couple of clients showed up, one right after another. It seemed like time for me to take off, too. But I waited till she had taken care of her business and then asked her one more thing that was on my mind.

"You yourself," I said, "would you say you liked Nelda a lot?"

"Sure I liked her a lot."

"Did she handle you just right?"

"How do you mean?"

"The way she handled men who liked her a lot. A friend but always professional?"

Now she saw what I meant. "I don't know why I should answer that," Wanda said.

"I don't know why either."

"You know something, Bethany?" she said, and I shrugged my shoulders a tiny bit to show I didn't. "You're pretty goddamned sharp, for a man."

7

GLADYS WILLIAMS HAD SAID TO MEET HER BY THE statue in Harvard Square, and I had asked what statue? Look around till you see a statue, she said. It'll be right next to the Out-of-Town Newsstand. And that's where the statue was—an ugly, graceless construction that jabbed into the air in an ugly, graceless way. How come there's never a Jesse Helms around when you really need one?

This hideous misuse of public funds must have been in my field of vision ten thousand times, and yet I didn't remember ever seeing it before. The mind protects us by airbrushing out power lines, street signs, telephone poles, and modern sculptures that would otherwise spoil our enjoyment of familiar scenes. I said as much to Gladys, who was waiting at our rendezvous.

"That's real deep," she said. "And real weird."

"Well, shit, Gladys, now I'm going to sulk all night."

"Okay, where we going to do it?"

"How about the Harvest?" I said. The Harvest was an overpriced yuppie joint, but it had a courtyard and I thought she might like it.

"How about the Bow and Arrow?" she said. "They got the same beer for half the price and nobody talks about real estate."

The Bow and Arrow is as downscale as you can get in the Harvard Square area. We took a table about half-way down the room, at a point equally distant from the jukebox and the TV.

"So listen, what should we talk about?" Gladys said when the waitress had our order for a pitcher of beer. "For instance, I saw this terrific show on Channel Two about otters. Want to talk about that?"

"Actually, no. I want to talk about how come you quit a good job cutting up corpses to comb out pubic hairs for the police department."

"You want to talk about me, is that it? My hopes, my fears, my dreams?"

"Sure. You show me yours, then I'll show you mine."

Gladys turned out to have been graduated from Lesley College after six years of combining study with work. Her job for the last two of those years had been as an assistant in Harvard's biology department, by which time it was too late to change her Lesley major in office administration or something. But a Harvard biology professor gave her free textbooks from his shelves full of publishers' samples, and let her sneak into lectures. By the time she had her bachelor's degree, he was willing to recommend her for a job in the pathology lab at Beth Israel. During her three years there and her two subsequent years with the Cambridge police, she had taken Harvard extension school courses in biochemistry, genetics, microbiology, immunology, neurobiology, endocrinology, and metabolism. Now she figured she was about ready for medical school.

"A Ph.D. is just as good for the kind of research I want to do," she said. "Or better. But with the M.D., you get twice the salary for doing the same research. So I'm laying out six hundred dollars for the Stanley Kaplan course this winter and I'll take the MCATs in February."

"Think you'll get into med school?"

"Why not? Look at all the assholes who did."

The reasoning she employed in her personal life was also impeccable. She lived alone, in a small apartment just off Kirkland Street. Most of the time she managed to have two boyfriends, each of whom she told about the other's existence. "First thing is it gives me a backup if one of them takes off or gets to be a pain in the ass," she said. "Also it keeps them on their toes if they know there's competition. They try just that little bit harder."

"How come everybody else has got to advertise for men in the *Phoenix* classifieds and you've got 'em two at a time?"

"You go after the shy ones. That's the easy part, finding them. They're grateful to be found. The trick, though, is knowing what to do with them once you've found them."

"Well, what?"

"Hey, I can't tell *you*. You're the wrong sex. You introduce your ladyfriend to me sometime and maybe I'll tell her."

By then we were on our third pitcher of beer. Pretty soon it would occur to Gladys that she was doing all the talking, at which point she might start asking all kinds of questions about me that I wasn't ready to answer yet. Not at this early stage of our acquaintanceship. To head this off, I told her about my conversation with the manager of Personal Leisure World.

"The thing that struck me," I said when I was done, "was that there seemed to be two totally different Emily Kellicotts. The one her father described to me was a pathetic, rebellious, undisciplined mess. The impression I got was she spent her whole life trying to embarrass her father."

"Well?" Gladys said. "Working at a massage parlor isn't exactly going to impress the shit out of his buddies at the faculty club, is it?"

"No, but nobody knew about her at the faculty club, either. She danced under another name, and she never talked about her folks, stoned or sober."

"She was a druggie, huh?"

"Actually, no. Wanda said maybe a line now and then if one of the girls offered her some, but nothing regular or serious."

"She drink?"

"Wanda said no, but her father said she was a lush and a druggie, both. Said every time he tracked her down she was either hammered or high. Screaming and hollering awful things at him. Very painful scenes."

"Maybe it made him more comfortable to think she was out of her head when she said the awful things."

"Maybe, but even shouting awful things doesn't sound like the Nelda they knew at the massage parlor. That woman was hardworking, reliable, pleasant, calm, popular with everybody, disciplined, in control of her life."

"Sounds like me, except for the pleasant and the popular."

"Actually it kind of does. Even to running the men in her life instead of letting them run her."

"You going to talk to this Pink Lloyd?"

"If I can find him."

"Pink Lloyd, Jesus. What's his last name?"

"Wales."

"Close enough."

"What do you mean?"

"You really don't know?" she said. "You never heard of Pink Floyd and the Wall? The rock group?"

"No."

"Hey, welcome aboard. This is the 1980s."

"Harrigan said the guy always wore pink shirts. I figured that was how he got the name."

"You must be in a time warp."

"Gladys, I feel so ashamed."

"You should." She topped off my beer and filled her own glass. She was keeping right up.

"Tell me more about this Wanda," she said.

"Lesbian in her early forties," I said. "Going to fat a little, but still not too bad a figure. She went to parochial school but didn't like it much. Probably dropped out young, ran away from home, something like that. Basically uneducated, but smart and perceptive. My guess is that she runs the place pretty well."

"Is it her place?"

"I doubt it very much. There'd be somebody else behind it, almost certainly."

"The mob?"

"Possibly. Not necessarily."

"Did you like her?"

"I kind of did, yeah. But then I don't have to work for her. My impression was that she wouldn't put up with much shit from the help."

"Tough, huh."

"Pretty tough."

"Tough enough to strangle a girl who held out on her?"

"And carve her male rival's initials into the girl as a little hint to the cops?" I said.

"For instance."

"I thought of that, but I don't like it much. The fact that she was naked. The semen. The hair you found."

"What do you like, then?"

"I don't have anything I like, really. Just questions."

"Here's another one for you, then," Gladys said. "How come she said her father died when she was thirteen?"

"To avoid talking about her family."

"Sure, maybe. But why thirteen?"

"Instead of twelve, or fifteen, or twenty-one? Where are you going with this?"

"I don't know, either. It's just another question. I thought of it because of my mother."

"She died when you were a kid?"

"She died, but only last year. I hadn't seen her in years, didn't want to, but I had to take care of getting her buried. I came across a medical history form she had filled out for the insurance company years ago, and she put down that she was hospitalized in 1960 for severe depression.

"Well, she was basically crazy and she had been put away three different times that I knew of, which she didn't list on the form at all. But I never heard of one in 1960. So I called my dad up in Portland, and sure enough, he said it never happened. That was one of her good years. She was locked up before and after, but not even close to 1960."

"The question being why she put down 1960 instead of 1957 or 1962?" I said. "Okay, what happened in 1960?"

"Her first child was born. Me."

"I get your point. I'll try to find out what happened when Emily was thirteen. I'm having dinner with her family tomorrow."

Meanwhile, though, the night was ahead of us. "What do you think?" I said. "Want to move on?"

142

"To where?"

"The Top Hat Lounge."

"You're still in that time warp, Bethany. There hasn't been a Top Hat Lounge in America since what? Maybe 1955?"

"It's a strip joint on Boylston Street. Emily used to work there. And Pink Lloyd hangs out there, according to Harrigan."

It turned out that the Top Hat, too, was in a time warp, just like Boston's whole Combat Zone. Chinatown was taking over the Zone, along with developers. I hadn't been down there for years, except for my visit to the dirty bookstore. Now, at night, it looked like a sad, near-deserted movie set. At the corner of Washington and Boylston was the China Trade Center, a shabby office building. A handful of pimps and petty thieves sprawled and slouched in the little open space in front of it.

"Whatever you want, man, I got it," offered one of them as we went by, but he seemed to be speaking his line by rote, like a telephone canvasser, without much hope of success. I didn't believe he really had it, any more than he did, and so we went on by. Video Peeps was closed and boarded up. Movies-Nude Photos was closed. Boston Bunnies was closed. Club 66, which had been sort of renowned in the old days, was closed. In the doorway lay two Cossack Vodka bottles, a bottle of Wild Irish Rose wine, a 7-Up can, and three paper napkins that had been used to blot up blood.

But down Boylston Street the Top Hat still hung on, no doubt preyed on by such minor parasites as cops, health inspectors, liquor inspectors, and bottom-rung mafiosi. The Top Hat's real enemies, and Chinatown's as well, were likely to be the politicians, bankers, developers, and lawyers who root for slops in the city's real estate market. Between them, they steal more on a slow day than the entire city bureaucracy does in a year. Soon enough they would gentrify the last of the hookers and sailors and Chinese waiters right out of the old Zone. Let Lowell or Quincy or some place take care of them; here, though, the yuppies are coming. With the eighteen-hundred-dollar-a-month condo payments that will leave nine tenths of them homeless and bankrupt when the national bill comes due. In ten years it will be hard to figure out how Reagan ever got elected by two land-slides, since not a one of the busted baby boomers will confess to voting for the man. Admitted Reaganauts will be found only in a handful of country clubs, protected from extinction by heavily armed bartenders, ball boys, and caddies. To the *pock, pock, pock* of the tennis balls, they will nap on the terrace and dream of the gone Gip-per, as their grandfathers dreamed of Warren Gamaliel Harding.

"Probably you're right," Gladys said when I finished explaining all this to her. "But right now, let's go on in. I've got to take a leak."

When you entered the Top Hat you were met right away by a wall—a baffle to keep the sidewalk traffic from getting a free peek at the show. Past this obstacle, a large man met us. "Table for two?" he said, like a real maitre d'.

"Maybe," I said. "We're looking for someone. Pink Lloyd?"

"Probably be in sometime," the large man said. "Prob-ably late."

"Any way to reach him?" I asked. "I got this girl here that wants to talk to him about a job. Only right now she's got to take a leak."

The large man looked Gladys up and down and ges-tured toward the rear.

"Okay tits," he said when she had gone. "Where'd you find her?"

"She's waitressing for me, I got a place over in Allston. She wants to make a little more money, you know?"

"There's somebody here that might know where Pink Lloyd is. Who should I tell him?"

"Tom Bethany. Just say Tom. Tom from Allston."

The big man took me to a table and disappeared out back. While he was gone, Gladys returned and a waitress came and took our order.

"I told him you were a waitress just like her," I said to Gladys as the woman left. "Only now you want to go for the big bucks, with Pink Lloyd."

"I don't know," Gladys said. "Would I have to go all the way?"

"I don't think so. My understanding is that most of them just want to talk."

"The hell with it then."

Our drinks came. Gladys had stuck with beer; I had broken my beer-only rule and ordered rye and Coca-Cola, out of a vague idea that rye and Coke was the thing to drink in a time warp. It was revolting.

The stage was a runway down the middle of the horseshoe-shaped bar. A light-skinned black girl, if such a thing can be, had just finished. The emcee invited us to give her a great big hand. Then we all settled down to a brief intermission, during which we were expected to drink our overpriced drinks and buy overpriced drinks for the bar girls.

"That would be the hard part, I'd think," Gladys said. "Look at that slimeball at the table over there. Can you imagine going up and talking to him?"

"I'd think the hard part would be getting up there naked."

"It would be for me. Not for her."

"How come?"

"I've got a fat ass and she didn't. Look, one of the police photographers is this repulsive creep that likes to take nude photos of girls. I asked him one time, I was curious, why would any girl take off her clothes for a repulsive creep like you? My exact words."

"Oh, I believe it."

"He didn't mind. Assholes like him, they think you're kidding. Anyway, what he told me he'd do is he'd walk up to the girls with the best bods on the beach and give them his card. The better the bod, the more likely she'd call him up."

"Makes sense, I guess."

"Sure it does. Look at you, the build on you. You telling me you'd be embarrassed to get up there in a male strip club? Let the girls stuff money in your jock?"

"I'd probably never do it, but you're right. I wouldn't feel embarrassed if I did."

"Naturally not. If you've got it, flaunt it."

"What about at the massage parlor? You think that'd be hard?"

"Why? You'd massage women, wouldn't you?"

"Some women I would."

"You'd do them all if it was your business. It only feels funny the first time or two. Ask a nurse or a hair-dresser, anybody that handles other people."

"They're not giving handjobs, though."

"Get a clue, Bethany. How big a deal do you think a handjob is?"

"Well . . ."

"Look, probably you never handled another man, so it seems weird. Doesn't seem so weird to us, though. You've got to bear in mind we've been doing it since ninth grade."

"Not with strangers."

"Everybody's a stranger at first. Besides, a handjob isn't really too personal, you know? In fact, it's what you do to a guy when you don't *want* to get too personal with him."

I was thinking that this seemed to make sense, too, when Pink Lloyd came up to our table. He wore a pink shirt and a pink handkerchief in his breast pocket. His jacket and pants were the color of coffee, very heavy on the cream. They were cut loose and floppy, in a fashion tradition dating all the way back to the early days of the Banana Republic. And on Pink Lloyd, to be honest about the thing, the look worked. He was slim, wide-shouldered, just short of six feet tall, and moved in the loose, bone-less, graceful way of a good tap dancer. He was the color that we whites spend the summer at the beach trying to reach, but never quite get to.

"Hey, how you doing?" he said, taking possession of the chair I waved him into. "Manny say this young lady looking around."

"Yeah, you could say."

"What's your name, honey?"

"Gladys."

"Well, we have to do something about that."

"Bullshit we do," said Gladys.

"Probably I ought to explain," I said. "The fact is, she's not looking for work. We're looking into the Kelli-cott murder."

Pink Lloyd looked at me without speaking for a moment. His eyes narrowed a trifle and the lines of his face hardened up. He reached into his mouth, tugged at something, and then laid a portable bridge down on the table, sharply enough to make a little click. Two teeth, attached to a device made of metal bands and pink plastic.

147

"I talked to you people already," he said. "Now I got to wear this."

"This is nothing to do with the police," I said. "We're working with the family on this." I passed him one of my Infotek cards. When he had looked it over, and looked me over some more, he handed the card back and put the bridge back in his mouth.

"Still it don't matter," he said. "Everything I said, you can get it from the police. I told the fuckers everything I know, can't help it if they didn't believe it."

"Well, they didn't," I said. "But I do."

"Then what do you want with me?"

"I want to find out about Emily herself."

"Emily?"

"Emily, Nelda. Where did she get Nelda from?"

"I guess 'cause it rhymed. The way she made Tony say, it was Nubile Nelda from Needham."

"Tony being?"

"The greaseball was just up there. The emcee."

"Nubile Nelda, huh?"

"Nubile meant like young stuff, way she told me."

"She wasn't from Needham, though."

"That was 'cause it rhymed, too. I axt her one time and she said it was just for fun, the whole name."

"But she used Nelda offstage, too?"

"Oh, yeah. Nobody knew no Emily. I didn't even know that myself till it come out in the papers."

"And you were pretty close to her, right?"

"Close as anyone."

"Which wasn't that close? Is that what you're saying?"

"It was and it wasn't. I'd see her sometimes and far as I know I was the only one that did. So that's why I say close as anyone."

"She didn't work for you, though? It wasn't that?"

"You knew her, you wouldn't even ask that question.

Even when I only saw her dancing here the first time, before I ever met her, it never even crossed my mind."

"Why not?"

"Shit, who knows? It's like when you're a kid, you know, when you go to robbing people on the street? You just get a feeling which ones ain't gonna fight back, which ones are. The way they move. Something."

"How did she move?"

"Like she was going somewhere all the time, and she was late."

"Somebody you could turn out, how would she move?"

"Different ways, but not like that. Lazy. You take your whore, mostly she's a lazy bitch. Move lazy, you know? Last thing you could say about Nelda."

"She worked at Leisure World, though."

"Not turning tricks."

"Pretty close, from what her boss says."

"Then her boss is giving you shit. Nelda done massages and that's it. She got through with you, it was like she took you apart and put you back together again. She didn't have to give you no more than a massage, and you got your money's worth."

"The manager said she gave handjobs to regular customers."

"Well, that could be, if she liked somebody and happened to feel like it." Pink Lloyd looked at Gladys, and said, "Any woman would do that, am I right?"

"If she liked somebody and felt like it?" Gladys said. "Sure, why not?"

"Sure. Don't make her a whore."

"You think there's any chance the manager could have killed her?" I asked.

"You know Wanda was hitting on Nelda?" I nodded. "Then you know she didn't get no place, either. If they had something going, maybe Wanda would have done it. Except it don't make sense."

"Why not?"

"Just don't. Nelda would have been too strong for Wanda. Besides, she had her clothes off."

And there it was again. What sense did it make for a woman to take her clothes off in a parking lot on a cold night?

"Did Nelda know anybody, any man, with a Spanish accent?" I asked.

"Not that I know of, unless it was somebody at work. Why? You think some spic did her?"

"Probably not, but a guy named Jose Soto came at me with a knife a few days ago and he wouldn't tell me why."

"I never heard that name, but that don't mean nothing. She knew plenty of people I didn't know."

"You didn't see that much of her?"

"Now and then is it. Used to be more when I first met her, but my bitches got jealous."

"You met her here, you said?"

"She was dancing, yeah. Sometimes she'd come over and sit with me between dancing so nobody wouldn't bother her, you know? The thing is, she wouldn't hustle drinks, told 'em that from the start."

"They didn't mind?" I asked.

"Don't matter if they minded. The body she had, they wanted her to dance more than they minded. Shit, Tony and them, they wanted to keep her picture outside even though she was dead."

"Why didn't they?"

"I told 'em. 'You sick fuckers,' I said, 'the girl's *dead*. You keep that picture out there, I bet you that guy Barnicle at the *Globe* would like to hear about it, put it in the paper.' I told them sick fuckers."

"Would they still have the picture?"

"I got it, you want to look at it. She had pictures of me, but I didn't have none of her. In fact that's how we happen to get it on, her pictures."

"How was that?"

"What happened, one night we was talking right at this table and she asked me would I model for her. I figured she was just coming on to me, you know, but it wasn't that. I went over to her place five or six afternoons before she finished the picture. Just sitting there while she would draw. But all the time we were talking, getting friendly, you know?"

"None of my business, but how long was it before you did get it on?"

"I'd say maybe a couple months."

"But it didn't last long because of your girls?"

"I wouldn't say it didn't *last* long. It lasted more or less up till she died, you know? Only there was a couple weeks there at first when we was seeing a lot of each other, and after it was whenever we could manage it, you understand what I'm saying?"

"I understand," I said, and actually I probably understood better than he wanted me to. It was looking to me as if Wanda had been right—that Emily had kept him on a string, for whenever she felt like a little custard cream pie à la mode.

"What happened to the pictures she made of you?" I asked.

"I guess her daddy took them when he cleared her place out."

"You ever meet him?"

"Not exactly. I seen him once."

"Where was that?"

"Right here. This dude came in and as soon as she spotted him she goes, 'Why, that fucker!' and runs up to him. She's hollering and the guy on the door comes over to see what's the trouble. You couldn't hear what she was saying on account of the music but then it stops and she's hollering, 'Get this son of a bitch out of here or I'm not going on!' Everybody's looking at the guy by now."

"He goes, does he?"

"Oh, yeah, he goes. She was pissed off you wouldn't believe. I never saw her like that, before or since."

"Was she drunk?"

"Sheeit. Know what she drank? Cream soda with a scoop of ice cream in it."

"How about drugs?"

"Somebody offer her some good coke she might take it or she might not. Mostly not."

"She tell you who the guy was after he left?"

"She had to dance first. Then she come back, told me it was her daddy wanting her to come home."

"She say why she didn't want to?"

"Wouldn't say another word about him. Till it come out in the paper I didn't know she was from around here, had a family, went to college, nothing. She didn't want to talk about it and you hadn't better ask her, neither."

The music came up so loud that we couldn't hear ourselves talking—a record or tape of some generic-brand bump-and-grind music. A girl with enormous breasts and thin legs came out, moving in vague relation to the beat. Except for the breasts, there was no point in watching her. We waited it out until it was time to clap, which I did loudly, out of pity rather than enthusiasm.

"Good tits on her anyway," Pink Lloyd said when the girl had bowed herself off the runway. "Can't dance for shit, though."

"How was Nelda?" I asked.

"She like something on the TV. She could *dance*. She'd put on this weird music, but she made it work, I'll say that for her."

"What kind of music?"

"From shows. She had this one about umbrellas and Rockefellers."

" 'Puttin' on the Ritz,' " Gladys said.

"Something," Pink Lloyd said. "She'd end up with this bow tie and a top hat on, like the Top Hat Lounge. Another one she'd come out with this miniskirt on and a kind of a round hat, came down over her ears. Song called the 'Viper Rag.' "

I didn't know that one; from her smile, Gladys did.

"She could've done real good as a dancer, no question," Pink Lloyd said. "I told her she ought to go to school for it. But couldn't nobody make her let go of that art shit."

We left before the next stripper came on. I drove conservatively, knowing that I wouldn't have a chance against a Breathalyzer. Nor would Gladys by now, so she wasn't much use as a designated driver.

"Fats Waller," she said. "That's who wrote 'Viper Rag.' Imagine playing stuff from *Easter Parade* and *Ain't Misbehavin'* for that crowd."

"I'm liking her more and more as we go along," I said.

"Me too. It must have tickled the shit out of her, dancing to those numbers. I'm surprised she didn't do 'Miss Otis Regrets.' "

"I got the distinct impression Pink Lloyd found his match when he met Emily, didn't you?"

"Lot more than his match," Gladys said. "I wonder what happened when he went out to Personal Leisure World that night. Suppose he was asking her for a date?"

"Probably close to it," I said. "I keep thinking of how it had to be that night, in the lot. Cold, raw, shitty."

"How do you know that?"

"I checked the weather in the papers for that day. Inside it's a regular night down at the massage parlor. Nothing special except a guy loses his nerve and walks out on Emily. Pink Lloyd comes in. He shoots the shit for a while. She walks him downstairs, says good night. How? Would she kiss him good night?"

"Might. Why didn't you ask him?"

"Hey, nobody's perfect. Okay, Pink Lloyd takes off. Emily goes back up. Joint closes. Emily leaves. Her car was found locked later on, so she never got to it."

"Probably."

"Okay, probably. Probably she got in somebody else's car, the weather the way it was."

"Or went back inside after Wanda closed up. Did Emily have a key?"

"She did, actually. She kind of ran things for Wanda whenever Wanda had to step out or took time off. But if it happened that way, why not just leave her body inside?"

"Or why not carry it outside and dump it in a snowbank so nobody would find it for a while? Makes as much sense as anything else."

"Not as much sense as if the guy dragged her into his car and raped her there."

"On the other hand, she doesn't sound like she would have been real easy to drag, does she?" Gladys said.

"No, definitely not too draggable."

"Not too undressable, either," Gladys said. It kept coming back to that.

I drove Gladys to her house and there was that awkward moment when each of you wonders what the other expects you to do. I was just drunk enough to want to, but just sober enough to know how dumb it would be. She must have been about the same, because we both looked at each other, and both started to laugh at about the same time.

She opened her door, got out, closed it, and looked in at me through the window. "I like you and I feel like it," she said. "You understand that, don't you?"

"Sure, I do. I like you and I feel like it, too."

"But we've each got our custard cream pie à la mode," Gladys said. She smiled and went up the walk to her door. Once she was safe inside I drove off—a little bit frustrated but mostly happy and relieved. Pieces of pie are everywhere, but it isn't every day you find a friend.

Thursday morning I woke up with a hangover, which used to happen to me a lot but doesn't so much anymore. I took a long, hot shower and then turned the cold on. Cold water in Cambridge in August is a long way short of icy, and it was a while till the top of my skull started to hurt from it. Then I repeated the hot-cold cycle twice. Sometimes, in mild cases, this takes care of a hangover. This wasn't one of those cases. I decided to run down to the corner for a *Globe* and then lie around in my air-conditioned bedroom until my head felt better. Which would have been around noon fifteen years ago, but would be more like four o'clock now.

And I would certainly have followed this program if I hadn't turned on the radio to catch the weather while I was shaving. It was going to be hot again—and police were trying to identify a corpse pulled from the Charles just after dawn. A sculler navigating through the fog downstream from the Weeks footbridge had bumped into what he at first thought was a floating log. The cause of the man's death was unknown pending results of an autopsy. "Police say the dead man may have been in a recent accident," the announcer said, "as his right arm was in a sling." I thought about that while I finished shaving, and then picked up the phone.

"This is your old pal, Tom," I said when the switchboard had finally put me through to Gladys Williams. "How do you feel?"

"I feel like shit, old pal. Which is exactly the way I hope you feel."

"Well, you get your wish. Listen, I'm sorry to bother you, but what do you know about the floater they pulled out of the river this morning?"

"That's part of why I feel so good. He was waiting when I got in this morning."

"Which arm was in the sling?"

"Right one."

"Had it been recently dislocated?"

"Could have been. There was edema, discoloration."

"What does he look like?"

"Late twenties, early thirties. White male, about five-nine, 160 or 165. Probably Hispanic."

"Shit."

"You know him?"

"I hope not, but I bet I do. Can I look at him?"

"Why not?"

His body cavity had been sewed back up after the autopsy with big, sloppy stitches. He looked a good deal like the man who had attacked me at Fresh Pond, although I could have been wrong. A corpse sometimes looks considerably different from the living person.

"The FBI should have his prints from the Immigration Service," I said. "If he's who I'm pretty sure he is, he's an immigrant from El Salvador named Jose Soto."

"Who is this guy, Tom?"

"He's the asshole who tried to kill me during the storm Tuesday. What happened to him?"

Gladys showed me the pathologist's report and interpreted where necessary. Death had been caused by drowning, but there was evidence of trauma to the trachea as well. He might have been choked into unconsciousness, and then revived enough in the water to gasp his lungs full of water. Or the choking might have had nothing to do with his drowning. His injured arm had been taped into immobility, and he could have panicked on hitting the water. Or maybe he just didn't know how to swim.

"Choked like Emily," Gladys said. "Shouldn't you talk to somebody here? They're not all like Harrigan. I can get you with Billy Curtin, the guy I told you about."

"I can call his office and tip them anonymously who this guy is," I said. "That'll keep you out of it. But I'd like to keep myself out of it, too. If I ever figure out what's going on, though, I'll find a way to let Curtin know."

"Yeah, well, be careful, Tom. It could be your neck. Literally."

"I do some wrestling," I said. "A lot of pretty good guys have had a crack at my neck."

" 'I do some wrestling,' " she mimicked. "Jesus, Tom, do men realize what assholes you sometimes sound like?"

"Some of us do," I said. "But we can't always help it."

8

"OR IF TONIGHT ISN'T CONVENIENT, I COULD DRIVE OUT to the Vineyard next week," I said. It was Friday night at the Kellicotts'. "Either way is fine."

"Lot of trouble for you," he said. "Might as well talk to them tonight while you're here. Save you the drive."

Kellicott raised his voice slightly, to include his wife and daughter in the conversation. They were across the large living room; Kellicott and I were at the bar, where he was fixing predinner drinks. "At some point Tom needs to talk to you ladies," he said.

"Yes, dear," said Susan Kellicott.

"Yes, Papa," said her daughter, Phyllis. I had never heard anyone call her father Papa before.

Phyllis needed a second glance. At first glance you got no clear impression of her. She was indistinct, like a half-erased drawing. You had to look again to see that she was one of those pretty girls who don't know that they're pretty. Her mother, on the other hand, had never been pretty and probably knew it all too well. She would have stood nearly as tall as her husband, but she stooped and her shoulders were hunched. She was bulky without having any definite shape. I tried to imagine what the Kellicotts had looked like as a young couple, in the light of Gladys's theory on couples balancing out.

Kellicott turned his attention back to me. "You're right to want to be sure," he said. "Teddy's wife, Gerry Ferraro's husband. You don't want these things coming up during a campaign."

That was certainly a reasonable, sophisticated reaction to a stranger's request for private interviews with your wife and your daughter. Personally I would have been irritated as hell and shown it. That was just another one of the reasons Kellicott was up for secretary of state and I wasn't. He didn't show it.

We joined the two women and talked for a few minutes about how hot it had been and when the gypsy moth caterpillars were due back and how people watered their lawns too much when the reservoirs were down. I had no very strong positions on any of these things; all I paid attention to was Mrs. Kellicott's behavior with her bourbon and water. She didn't seem to be going at it in any great haste, but the drink was gone before the ice cubes had lost their squareness. She didn't bother her husband for a refill; she went over to the sideboard and took care of herself. I recognized the pattern, which had been mine for long enough and on occasion still was. A glass left empty, even momentarily, disrupted the proper order of things.

"When are we going in, dear?" Kellicott asked when his wife rejoined us.

"I told Bridget seven," she said, "but it doesn't really matter. Everything's cold."

"Twenty minutes or so till we sit down, then," Kellicott said to me. "Would that be time enough for you to get started?"

It probably would. I decided to talk with Phyllis first, on grounds that I would probably need more time with her mother. We went into a small study, lined with bookshelves, off the living room. Phyllis left half of her gin and tonic behind her on the sideboard. I took my drink in with me. It was straight tonic, not because I cared about keeping a clear head, but because Kellicott hadn't had any beer. Beer was all I usually drank, anymore.

I explained the kinds of things I had to ask her, and why, and then, when she seemed resigned enough, I set out. In a small voice, managing to sound cooperative and offended at the same time, she said she didn't very much like the taste of liquor, she had never experimented with drugs, had never been arrested, had never been under treatment for any psychological or emotional problem, never been expelled from school, been pregnant, hospitalized, ticketed for a moving violation, addicted to any substance, affiliated with any organization advocating the overthrow by force or violence of the United States, and so on and so forth.

"Well, that takes care of it," I said at last, and then went on to ask her about the only thing so far that really made me curious about her. "I notice you call your father Papa," I said.

"Isn't that all right?" she said.

"Oh, sure. I just never heard it before, is all."

"We called him Papa when we were little, and I guess I just kept on."

"Did Emily keep on?"

"Not once she got bigger, no. She called him A.K."

"Like the rifle."

"Rifle?"

"There's an assault rifle called the AK-47."

"No, it was his initials."

"Oh, right," I said, cutting my losses. It's tricky dealing with somebody who's totally humorless. "A kind of a nickname. I guess they were pretty close?"

"Papa loved her very much."

"And presumably she loved him?"

"Emily was a very cold person."

I waited, and waited. Until she felt she had to explain herself.

"It wasn't her fault. She was very young."

"Do I have it wrong? I thought she was your older sister."

"She was. I don't mean young in that way."

"Young in what way?"

"Always taking. Never giving. I shouldn't be saying these things. I don't want to talk about my sister. It's over for her, but we still have each other. Our family. We're alive and we have to take care of each other."

She stopped talking and sat there, her hands working and working at one another.

"Well," I said, "I guess we must be about ready to go in." I had never heard anyone use the expression "going in" before, in the sense that Papa had. "Incidentally," I asked, "what do you call your mother?"

"Mummy," Phyllis said.

Nobody I knew had ever called their mother Mummy, either.

Dinner was cold, as Susan Kellicott had warned us. But it wasn't just stuff out of the refrigerator. We started with vichyssoise so good it was obvious I had been served counterfeits up till then. "Oh, Bridget probably

had some of that old duck stock still around," Mrs. Kellicott said. Duck soup.

Then we had a macédoine of vegetables, steamed,
chilled to crispness, and dressed with olive oil and vine-
gar. The main course was cold lobster meat, tails and
claws. To go with it, Bridget served each of us a small
bowl of freshly made mayonnaise, bright yellow and
glistening. Dessert was sliced peaches with whipped
cream. It was the best meal I had eaten in a long time,
perhaps ever, which I told Bridget as she was clearing
away.

She jerked her head in the direction of the kitchen
and said, "I'll tell Otto you liked it."

"Otto is Swiss," Mrs. Kellicott said when Bridget had
gone. "The Swiss are beautifully trained."

Otto and Bridget could be a complication.

"Do they go with you to the Vineyard?" I asked.

"Oh, yes. We do a good deal of entertaining there, you
know. Bridget and Otto will drive down tonight as a
matter of fact, so they can go over first thing tomorrow
and open the house." And so they wouldn't be a complication at all.

At dinner we had talked some more about the heat,
and about the Vineyard, and parking problems in down-
town Cambridge, and how the best way to keep silver
looking good was to use it every day. The silver did look
good, too: simple, graceful utensils with their mono-
grams worn to soft illegibility by countless polishings.

My interest was in how the members of the little family acted around each other, and in how Emily might
have fitted into those patterns. The Kellicotts gave few
clues, though; perhaps they never did, with an outsider
present. The father was polite and deferential toward
the mother; the daughter was polite and respectful
toward both parents; the mother was polite and slightly

withdrawn. She carried along the conversation compe-
tently but absently, the way a person might drive one-
handed on the interstate, her thoughts far away. Neither
woman seemed stupid, although neither seemed particularly smart, either. This meant nothing, though, particularly where women were concerned. In America, for
women even more than for men, intelligence is a
weapon to be carried concealed.

After dinner I excused myself and went to the small
bathroom off the entrance hall. There I set to work. With
the few small things I had brought with me, I backed
out the screws from the bottom half of the window latch,
replacing them with screws that were a size too small
for the holes. I cracked the screen just far enough open
so that the latches on each side were unable to seat, and
slid a broken twig under the screen to hold it up. Then
I closed the window so that it appeared locked, and
rejoined the company.

I would just as soon have gone on talking about the
servant problem or something, since I wasn't looking
forward to my interview with Susan Kellicott. Her background, unlike those of her daughter and her husband,
actually did create problems for the Kellicott appointment. She knew it and I knew it and Kellicott knew it.
Even Phyllis probably knew it, although her mother's
psychiatric and medical history may have been kept
from her. It was a dirty job but it had to be done, as Ted
Bundy no doubt used to say to himself before squaring
his shoulders and getting on with it. To Mrs. Kellicott,
I said, "Well, shall we get it over with?"

We used the same room where Phyllis and I had
talked. "I'm sorry about all this," I said. "It's no fun for
me, and even less for you."

Susan Kellicott nodded. I remembered her daughter's
nervously twisting hands. The mother's hands lay

motionless in her lap. As far as appearances went, she was just waiting for her caller to get on with whatever he had on his mind. Fine.

"Your husband said you had a rough time when you were younger."

"That's true."

"Were drugs involved?"

"Drugs weren't such a big thing in those days."

"So the answer is no?"

"I smoked a marijuana cigarette in Paris with a boy I was seeing then. Or he said it was marijuana. It didn't seem to me that it did anything."

"And that's it, for drugs?"

"Except for prescription drugs, yes."

"Which prescription drugs?"

"I've had Librium prescribed. And Valium."

"Was that for depression?"

"Depression, yes."

"Would you have any objection if I talked to your doctors?"

"I thought they weren't supposed to do that."

"They're not, unless you give them permission. Even then, they might not."

"You could talk to Dr. Peterson, I suppose. Dr. Wiley and Dr. Milmine are dead."

"What kind of doctors are they? Were they, I guess?"

"Nervous disorders. Specialists in that sort of thing."

"Psychiatrists?"

"I don't know. Not with couches and things, certainly. Father would never have stood for that." I guessed he never would have stood for a Jew treating his daughter, either. Peterson, Wiley, and Milmine. It must have been tough finding three Gentile psychiatrists.

"Are you still Dr. Peterson's patient?"

"I see him occasionally. He's right here in Cambridge."

"What would he tell me if I talked to him?"

"I don't know what he'd say. How could I know?"

"Would he say that he currently writes you prescriptions for Librium and Valium?"

"Valium only."

"On a daily basis?"

"Oh, no, not nearly. Not for years. They don't think as highly of Valium as they used to, you know."

"I have to ask these things, you understand, Mrs. Kellicott . . ."

"Oh, I understand."

"The campaign has to be ready in case the Republicans get hold of it and put it out, the way they did with the Eagleton business. Senator Markham's people have to be able to say they knew all about it, it's ancient history, so on and so forth. Conceivably even put it out themselves as a preemptive strike. Your husband can tell you."

"He has."

"Then you know what I have to ask. Any electroshock?"

"Twice, when I was a girl."

"Suicide attempts?"

"The same thing. Twice. I took sleeping pills. Dr. Milmine said they weren't serious attempts."

"Cries for attention?"

"How did you know he called them that?"

"I didn't, but that's what they always call taking pills. Unless it works."

"Really? I thought it was a phrase he came up with himself. My feelings were hurt because he didn't take me seriously. Of course I was just a child."

"Maybe he did take you seriously. Were the two courses of electroshock therapy after the two attempts?"

"Not too long after. While I was ill."

"Maybe you stopped trying to kill yourself because you were afraid he'd shock you again if you did."

"I never thought of that."

"I doubt if he did, either. Shock treatment was just the fashion in those days, like tonsillectomies."

"Tonsillectomies?"

"Nothing. Just thinking aloud. Anyway, the most anybody could conceivably come up with, it would be these things years ago. Before your marriage?"

"Oh, yes. Both of them."

"Nothing since?"

"No, nothing. Sometimes I go away for a rest, sometimes."

"Where's that?"

"Different places. Cherry Plains. Hartford Retreat."

"When was the last time?"

"Oh, years. Maybe last year."

"Mrs. Kellicott, I want to tell you something. I drink now, to some extent. But I used to drink a lot. Day in and day out, a lot. So the people I'd be around, they'd mostly be drinkers, too. For years that's mostly who I knew, people who drank. What I'm saying is we understand each other."

"Maybe we do."

"How early do you start?"

"At lunch."

"I used to keep it in my bureau. You?"

"In the blanket chest."

"Do you ever get drunk?"

"I suppose it depends what you mean by that."

"Blackouts, passing out, throwing up, not making sense when you talk, stumbling or falling down."

"Heavens, no."

"So you're like me, a good drinker. Good drinkers don't do those things. You learn what your dose is and you keep yourself up to it. The dose goes up as you develop tolerance, so other people sometimes think you're a drunk. But that's because they'd be drunk if they took your dose."

"I never thought of it that way."

"I used to function just fine, whenever I wanted to. If I decided I didn't want to, I just went over my dose. You function fine, too. I was watching you. Nobody would know but another drinker."

"Will it hurt Alden that I drink?"

"I doubt it very much. Mrs. Eisenhower and Mrs. Ford drank, and it never hurt their husbands. It's just something the campaign needs to know, in case."

The easy part was over. Now for the hard part. "The other thing they need to know, Mrs. Kellicott, is about Emily."

"Emily? Why Emily?"

"It's just a loose end, is all."

"But that man did it. The man who was using her. They just couldn't prove it, Alden said, but they know."

"They could be right, but the thing is that officially it's still open. So I have to find out all I can. Did you see much of Emily after she dropped out of college?"

"I never saw her, not once. She called me every year on Mother's Day. If Alden answered, she'd hang up and call again until I was the one who picked up."

"What did she say?"

"Just that she was fine, and not to worry. To take care of Phyllis. They were short conversations, just a minute or two."

"Did you ask where she was, what she was doing?"

"Not after the first time, no. She made it very clear it wasn't any of my business."

"Was she hostile?"

"Not hostile, no. She couldn't be bothered to show that much emotion to a mere mother."

Susan Kellicott had been talking the way I had driven the night before—so practiced at being drunk that she mostly seemed sober. But let a child dart into my headlights and the liquor would have shown itself, no doubt of it. It had shown itself in Mrs. Kellicott just then, at the thought of Emily's calls on Mother's Day. I sat without saying anything, knowing she would go on. When she did, it was in the unsteady voice of someone trying to avoid tears.

"You don't know what to do, you just don't. You try to raise them the way everybody says you should raise them and they hate you. Not hate, hate would be better. Contempt. Pathetic. They think you're pathetic. Maybe they're right. How can we know why they think these things? How in God's name can we know?"

I made a gesture with my hands to show that I didn't have the answer, either. As indeed I didn't. To look at the question with uncomfortable honesty, contempt had certainly been part of what I felt for my own parents. Perhaps my distant daughter, off in Alaska, felt contempt for me. What had Kellicott felt for his father, the estate chauffeur?

"She was such a sweet, sunny child," Mrs. Kellicott said. Now her voice was frankly out of control, and her eyes were shining with tears. One ran down her cheek and she brushed at it, not bothering to hide it.

"She'd sit on Papa's lap and he'd pretend to pull her little braids and she'd pretend to be hurt, and then she'd laugh and laugh."

"This is your father?"

"Emily's father. Alden. When the children came, I got into the habit of calling him Papa."

"Was that what you called your father?"

"As a matter of fact it was, yes."

"When did she stop laughing?"

"I don't see ... Oh, Emily. It was the summer she went off to canoeing camp in Maine. They saw bears and moose, and she learned how to cook some kind of awful oatmeal bread they ate. There was never a clue in her letters that anything was wrong. She sounded like her same old self. All the counselors and the other campers wrapped right around her little finger, according to her. But Alden noticed right away that she was different, when he went up to drive her back."

"In what way?"

"Well, she was always a strong-willed, self-determined little thing, and God knows she still was. But it turned into a rebelliousness, almost a hatefulness. The sweetness was gone. The sunniness was gone. You read so much these days, those poor children on the milk cartons. Back then you didn't hear so much about it."

"You think she was abused or molested somehow at the camp?"

"Well, she wasn't that way before. The first time Alden noticed the change in her was when he was driving her back down."

"Did you ask her whether anything had happened?"

Her fingers got busy with the collar of her blouse. "I was away at the time," she said.

"Away ..."

"Hartford ... the Hartford Retreat."

"Did your husband ask her?"

"Alden tried. They had always been very close. But she told him nothing at all had happened."

"Were they close after that?"

"She wasn't close with anybody after that summer. She completely changed. She lost interest in school. She dropped her old friends and she didn't bring her new friends around the house, if she even had any. She had been a wonderful little field hockey player, but she gave it up entirely. The only thing she took any interest in was drawing."

"What did she draw?"

"She would never show anybody, but one time she left out something she had been working on. It was a meadow full of flowers, with a lawn mower up front. An old-fashioned hand mower, just standing there. Somebody had mowed part of the meadow, and the jonquils and daffodils were lying on the ground, all cut off and just lying there."

"How old was Emily?"

"Let's see, I came across the drawing when I was getting her things together for spring break. That was the year we went to Bermuda over the spring break . . . Fifteen, going on sixteen."

"I meant when she went to the camp."

"Oh. That was the summer she was thirteen."

When I was a high school student in Port Henry, New York, we still wrestled on the old canvas mats. The mats were hard, but the worst was the canvas itself. All season you'd be covered with what the cyclists call road rash, big patches of cracking scab where the canvas had rubbed the skin off your elbows, your knees, your ears, your nose. If you wrestled long enough, you'd probably have been worn smooth like a stone in a stream.

Now it was better. The floor of Harvard's wrestling room was covered wall to wall with thick foam rubber with a smooth surface that went relatively easy on your skin. And the foam itself soaked up a lot of the impact when you smacked into it. The top of my head was socketed into the thick mat as comfortably as you could expect, considering that my skull was supporting half my body weight. The other half was on my feet. Everything else was arced into the air as I held my bridge. I was looking upside down at a sign running along one wall. It read EARNING THE RIGHT TO WIN BEGINS HERE.

I kept the strain on my neck muscles as long as I could and then rolled my weight forward until my body pivoted over my head in a sort of backward somersault with no hands. I wound up on my hands and knees, facing in the opposite direction. One drop of sweat followed another off the point of my chin, and made spots on the crimson mat. Soon the spots ran together into a wet blotch. No one bothered to air-condition the wrestling room during the summer. No one was expected to be in it, but I had a key and one of the duplicate staff ID cards I get every year from some underpaid teaching assistant in exchange for paying his gym fees. The privacy meant that I could perform bizarre drills—like the one I had just finished—without worrying whether non-wrestlers in the public exercise room thought I was showing off, or crazy. I had been at it since nine in the morning. Now it was close to eleven, and the sun was coming in strongly.

I stayed on my hands and knees for a few moments, letting my heart and my breathing slow down. Then, not bothering to get up, I crawled over to the two throwing dummies lying against the wall, one on top of the other. Their limbs ended in stumps, as if the hands and legs had been burned off. The arms stuck out stiffly in front, and somebody had jammed one dummy down on top of the other so that they were spending the summer locked in congress. I leaned back against them, folding my arms and closing my eyes while my system settled back to normal. I saw the Kellicotts at dinner, eating with their old and beautiful silver off new and beautiful bone china by Pfaltzgraff. There had been something at dinner that reminded me of something. What, though, and of what?

Three quarters of an hour later, the heat in the airless room woke me up. My T-shirt and shorts were still as sweat-soaked as they had been when I fell asleep. The top dummy was dark with sweat where my cheek had lain against it. I was still half in my dream, a dream from my time in Alaska. Judy Purvis was there, and her husband, Ham, who had had half the women in town sniffing around after him hopefully. Now and then their hopes were realized, too, which Judy probably knew. In the dream Ham was going out the door into a storm and she was looking after him the way she always did when he didn't know her eyes were on him. Beyond any possible misunderstanding, the look said I love you, and it said something terribly sad besides. It also said I know perfectly well you don't love me back, but after all, who could?

That was what I had been trying to remember about dinner at the Kellicotts': where I had seen that kind of look before, the look that Susan Kellicott gave her husband when she thought she was unobserved.

9

SATURDAY AFTERNOON PHIL JEFFERS WAS IN WITH THE senator and couldn't see me just yet. That's what Arthur Kleber told me, and so I told Arthur that Phil specifically said 2:00 P.M., and here it was 2:00 P.M.

"You want to bust in on the candidate, go ahead," Arthur said. "I can't stop you." He thought about that for a moment.

"I'd have to try though, wouldn't I?" he said. "Shit."

"Don't worry, Arthur," I said. "I won't bust in on the candidate. Him and Phil are probably having one of those top-level strategy sessions, right?"

Arthur shrugged. Maybe they were dissecting frogs in there, or saving the rain forest, or amending the constitution of South Dakota. He didn't care.

"You pick out your embassy yet, Arthur?"

"I should live so long."

"Things not going so good, huh?"

"Put it like this, okay? This guy, you kick him in the balls, he goes, 'Hey, listen, I'm sorry. Did my balls get in your way? Does your foot hurt?' "

"Are you saying he's a gentleman?"

"Well, it's not quite that bad. But I'd say he was in the wrong business, definitely yes."

Just then the man in the wrong business came out of Jeffers's office. He was closely followed by Jeffers and two other aides.

"You remember Tom Bethany," Jeffers said, on the assumption that the senator didn't.

"Certainly," Senator Markham said, sticking out his hand. He sounded as if I had never been far from his thoughts. "How have you been, Tom?"

I took his hand in mine and covered both our hands in a warm grip with my left hand, just firmly enough so that he wouldn't execute the rest of his maneuver. Which would have been to move on without a break in his stride, trailing a "Nice to see you again" behind him.

"Just fine, Senator," I said when I had brought him to a halt. "Coming up with some stuff you ought to know about."

"Good, wonderful," he said. "That's the way. Tell Phil about it, will you?"

And I let him go, having given it a try. "Nice to see you again," the senator said over his shoulder, moving on with his two aides. Phil Jeffers stayed behind and gestured me into his office.

"What was that shit all about?" he asked when we were alone. We both know what shit he meant. A courtier's main business is keeping anybody else from speaking directly to his prince.

"What shit?" I nevertheless said.

"What shit?" he mimicked. "You were covering your

174

ass in case it turns out later that Kellicott was butt-fucking Mary Poppins or something."

He had lost me, but just for the instant it took to pretend I was him. Then I saw what he had seen. If I missed anything big on Kellicott and it later blew up in the campaign's face, Jeffers would be figuring I had just arranged matters so that I could claim I told him but he never passed it on.

"Actually, Phil, I just wanted to find out whether your guy has enough brains to reach past you for his information."

"Bullshit."

"And he doesn't."

"You tell me anything that amounts to shit, it'll get to him. What have you got?"

"That's just it. Nothing that you'd figure amounts to shit. That's why I wanted to give Markham a chance to hear it."

"Well, he blew his chance. So what have you got?"

"I had dinner at Kellicotts' last night."

"You told me you were going to. So what happened?"

"She's a lush, his wife."

"No crime, as long as she can carry it."

"Oh, she can carry it."

"So let her."

"His daughter, the one that died? She was a good kid. Had it all together."

"And?"

"And Kellicott says she was a mess."

"Plenty of people don't know their own kids."

He had me there. I didn't know my own kid, either.

"Usually they get it the other way around, though," I said. "They pretend a bad kid is a good kid."

"Sometimes yes, sometimes no." He had me there, too. As soon as I had said the words, I knew they were

wrong. Plenty of parents think perfectly good kids are
bad kids. Still, something smelled wrong to me about
the murder of Kellicott's daughter and I was being paid
to try to make Jeffers smell it, too. So I went on, without
much hope.

"The point here, Phil, is that the case is still open."

"What are you telling me? Kellicott has to put his
whole career on hold because the cops can't find out
who killed his daughter?"

"It's just something that could come down on you
someday, that's all."

"Like one of those pianos that fall on guys in the car-
toons? You ever hear about a piano that actually fell on
a guy?"

"There's a piano up there. That's all I'm telling you."

"Not enough. Tell me something else."

"A guy tried to kill me."

"A guy? What guy?"

"A guy named Jose Soto. From El Salvador. He wound
up dead in the Charles, full of water."

"Oh, Jesus, no . . . Bethany, what kind of shit have
you dumped us into?"

He must have been feeling the way Haldeman and
Ehrlichman felt when E. Howard Hunt's name turned
up in connection with a third-rate burglary in a place
called the Watergate. Jeffers relaxed when I explained
that I hadn't killed Soto; Soto had only tried to kill me.

"What's it got to do with anything?" Jeffers said when
I had finished. "I mean a Hispanic tries to mug you, you
see it in the papers all the time." Jeffers said Hispanic
the way Billy Carter used to say Negro, so you knew
what he'd rather say.

"I was wearing shorts and a twelve-dollar Casio," I
said. "What was he mugging me for?"

"How do I know?"

"It was a jogging path and he followed me there in a thunderstorm," I said. "Get real, Phil."

"All right, let's get real. A guy you never saw before tries to kill you. Nobody else ever saw the guy before, either."

"The sanctuary guy saw him before."

"That's nobody. Nothing ties him to Kellicott, nothing ties him to you. He tried to kill you, I'm sorry. But it's your worry, not ours."

"You don't think he's got anything to do with that piano?"

"Give me a break with the pianos, okay?"

"Up to you. You're paying for it, I'm giving you what I've got."

"So far you've got just what we hoped you'd have, Bethany. Nothing."

"Will you tell Markham about it?"

"About nothing? Why?"

"I'll send you a report, then."

"Don't. Nothing on paper. You held the guy upside down and shook him and nothing came out. Fine. Now wrap it up."

"I hired on by the week, so you're still entitled to today and Sunday. There's one other thing I thought I'd look into."

Jeffers waved his hand to say go ahead and look, be my guest.

The night was so dark that only the outlines of the Kellicott house showed from the street. But from my invited visit the night before, I knew that it was a two-story clapboard house, painted white with black shutters. Enormous maples rose higher than the tall brick chimneys on the four corners of the Kellicott house. The grounds, big enough to hold three or four smaller houses, took up the middle of the short block. The property was enclosed by a six-foot picket fence with gates standing open at either end of a semicircular driveway. A mounting block stood in the middle of the semicircle, where carriages once discharged visitors. Four steps led from the cobblestoned driveway up to a small portico. There was a fanlight over the front door. The entrance was lit by a lamp that hung from the ceiling of the portico, giving an impression of occupancy. But in theory the family and the servants were safely on Martha's Vineyard.

In theory, too, I knew perfectly well that most burglars don't get caught. But in the here and now, I also knew perfectly well that unseen neighbors were wondering what I was doing on their quiet street. Certainly the people next door could see me from their windows, even though clouds covered the moon and I was creeping along the hedges that bordered the drive. Certainly their dogs could smell me and would bark any minute. The people across the street would see me now as I left the bushes and went out onto the open lawn quickly but casually, as if I belonged. They'd know, of course, that I didn't. They'd be dialing 911 right now. Reporting that I was in the shadows along the side of the house, raising the bathroom window . . . hoisting myself up to the sill . . . disappearing inside.

I slid the window shut behind me and listened to the dark house. Only a hum was in the air—and then it stopped. I thought of some sort of burglar alarm, before I got a grip and thought of the air-conditioning system shutting off. There's no better way to slow down time than to listen with every nerve for noises in somebody else's house at night. An hour or so passed in perhaps thirty seconds, but nothing broke the silence except the tiny sounds of internal housekeeping—my own breathing and my own pulse in my ears.

I began to move one slow foot in front of the other, picking up courage with each step that went unchallenged. In a minute or two it was hard to remember what all the fuss had been about, and I was making my way along with only the normal caution of somebody in a dark and unfamiliar place. When I had reached the hallway the moon came out from behind the clouds so that I could see well enough, my eyes having got used to the darkness by then. This was all to the good; I didn't dare turn on any lights for fear that the neighbors might know the house was supposed to be empty over the weekend. My plan, in fact, was to find some place to sleep upstairs and to go exploring seriously only when the sun came up. I was heading for the stairs when it happened.

A crash of music came from behind me—the discord of notes struck at random, followed by an awkward riffling of keys from the piano in the drawing room. Another time and another place, the sound would have been unremarkable. Just then it taught me that fight or flight aren't the only two options when danger explodes in the hunter-gatherer's face. He can also stand paralyzed, which was the choice my system made for me.

After that single harsh musical phrase came nothing, no whisper of noise, nothing at all. I stood forever, or so it seemed, without moving. Once before I had been frozen with fear like this, one time rock climbing in the Aleutian range. I had got myself in a kind of cup on the face of a cliff in the Valley of Ten Thousand Smokes, with a two-hundred-foot sheer drop before me and an unclimbable incline behind me. The same fear immobilized me then, until at last I worked it through my head that I had just climbed down the unclimbable incline after all. And now I would damned well have to make myself climb back up if I didn't want to die there on the rock face.

I didn't want to die with one foot on the bottom step of Kellicott's stairway, either, and so I had just about decided to head toward the drawing room when a cat came out of it.

"Fucking cat," I said aloud, sounding mean to myself.

The cat, indifferent, padded off down the hall silently. Pretty nearly the only time you can hear a cat walking is when the damned thing jumps onto a keyboard.

Upstairs at last, and my heart slowed down somewhat, I examined the Kellicotts' living arrangements. There were four bedrooms on the second floor. The windows of the large master bedroom gave out on the gardens in back of the house. Under bright lights instead of dim moonlight, it would have looked like a boudoir display in a very expensive store. Flower patterns and puffy comforters and down pillows and ruffles were everywhere. Rugs and fabrics and wallpaper seemed to be in various shades of pale gray, but probably in daylight they would turn out to be pastel.

It reminded me of Hope's separate bedroom in Washington, which gave the same impression of overwhelming femininity. You felt like an intruder into some secret, perfumed place where no men, or few, had ever been allowed entrance before. I imagined Mrs. Kellicott lying propped up on these pillows, wearing a satin peignoir, watching the large TV that sat on a table at the foot of her bed. Did she have a remote control so that she wouldn't have to get out of bed except for bodily functions?

I left and moved down the hall.

The bedroom next door was that of a teenage girl, with school banners and posters of male rock stars on the wall. It had a look of unnatural and temporary order about it, like a room that will only stay neat until the occupant returns from freshman year in college. But the occupant would never return. On the wall was a framed diploma from Buckingham, Browne & Nichols School. I took it to the window and read the hand-lettered name in the moonlight: Emily Milton Kellicott.

Alden Kellicott's room was around the corner. It was part office and part bedroom. Bookcases ran around all four walls, interrupted only by the windows and the two doors. The door to my left stood half open, showing a bathroom sink with a mirror over it. A bed sat to my right, pushed up against the bookshelves. In front of the windows there was a massive desk of carved mahogany. The computer sitting on the antique desk should have clashed with it, but somehow didn't. Nor did the space-age telephone with the elaborate console. Another, smaller telephone was on a table next to an armchair opposite the bed. The room was also equipped with a bureau, a second armchair, a couple of low, two-drawer oak filing cabinets, and a small refrigerator camouflaged to look like another oak cabinet. An expensive German coffee machine sat on top of it.

The room seemed to have been assembled for utility rather than show. The carpeting underfoot felt like some durable indoor-outdoor stuff. The furniture seemed to have been plunked down wherever it would be handy. A portable TV sat on one of the filing cabinets. No photographs or anything of a personal or family nature stood on the bureau, or on the unused portions of the bookshelves. There was no closet in the room, which made me curious enough to poke around till I found sliding doors in the hallway outside; in them I felt his suits and jackets, hanger after hanger, dozens of them.

Back in the bedroom I opened the refrigerator, risking

the brief and slight illumination. Inside were two bottles of white wine, one full and one half gone, and a six-pack of club soda. Kellicott could have afforded Perrier by the shipload, but he seemed to have enough sense not to do it when he could get the same absence of flavor at a quarter of the price in a fine domestic water.

His bathroom had what looked like light-tight shutters on the windows. I closed them and turned on the light. The bathroom was huge, the size of a large bedroom. Perhaps that was what it had once been. Now it was where Kellicott kept his expensive toys. A sauna was built into one end. Next to it was a glass-enclosed shower stall with six shower heads installed at different heights and angles, from overhead down to knee level. Thick, fluffy towels, big enough to serve as sheets, hung from chrome racks along the wall. A bidet was next to the toilet. I wondered about that. Piles? A Nordictrack exerciser and a Concept II ergometer stood side by side on the black tile floor, and an exercising device with pulleys and chromed weights was folded up against the wall. The walls themselves were dark green with white trim; on them hung silver-framed prints of Victorian vintage. There was an alcove with mirrors on three sides, the sort they have in tailor's shops that lets you check the fit from all sides.

I might have added parallel bars for dips and a chinning bar, and perhaps a foam-rubber exercise mat instead of the deep-piled white throw rugs. Apart from those small additions, Kellicott's facilities struck me as just about perfect. He even had a set of straight razors, a shaving mug, a huge badger-hair brush, and a strop hanging by the sink. Learning to shave with a straight razor, like learning to play the trumpet, is one of those things I'll never do and always regret that I didn't.

The last bedroom was Phyllis's. It was less grand than

her mother's, but very much along the same lines. Delicate, costly, nondurable, decorative. Frills and femininity. The only sign that a child must once have lived there was a doll, which was perched not on the pillows but on a windowsill. For the rest it was a woman's room, not a girl's. There was even an old-fashioned ladies' writing desk, and a boudoir settee of the type that lets you lean against one end while your feet hang off the other. Or mine would, anyway.

Of the four bedrooms, Phyllis's struck me as the least uncomfortable, speaking psychologically rather than physically, for me to sleep in. I locked the door to avoid further surprises from the damned cat, got undressed, and slid under the light down comforter. It was just about the right degree of covering, with the air-conditioner maintaining a steady seventy or so.

I had established a line of retreat before turning in—out the window, onto the roof of a rear porch, and an easy drop into the geraniums. But the thought still stayed with me that I would be in very bad trouble in a number of ways if I got caught breaking and entering. I lay awake worrying about that, until my thoughts turned at last to the life that must be lived on this floor.

The upstairs rooms told a clear story. Mrs. Kellicott, the former Susan Milton, lived alone in what amounted to an elaborate private ward, self-medicating herself with alcohol and, perhaps, whatever drugs she could talk the doctors out of. Her husband had long since moved out of the sickroom and built a retreat of his own.

I imagined how evenings must be in the Kellicott home. Emily, the life and vibrancy of the family, gone for years and now dead. Mrs. Kellicott, disappearing upstairs after dinner to her drugs, booze, and television. Alden Kellicott disappearing to write or read in his bedroom-study, or to exercise in his miniature health club. I wondered if Mrs. Kellicott ever set foot in his territory, or he in hers.

Did Phyllis stay downstairs in the evenings or did she disappear, too, up to this room? I thought of Phyllis, pretty but not knowing it. Young, but old in her manner. Perhaps she was the mother in the house, and her mother the child? What did she do up here, in her grown-up's bedroom, with no books, no TV, no stereo? Did she sew? Knit? What?

I let the birds wake me, before the sun was up. I shaved and brushed my teeth in Phyllis's bathroom, and then I began my daylight search of the big house by climbing up to the attic. As attics go, the Kellicotts' seemed practically sterile: a few pieces of unused furniture, empty luggage, six new-looking footlockers full of blankets and linens and smelling of mothballs. The only clutter was in a corner set aside for the artifacts of childhood. It held field-hockey sticks, toys, picture books, dollhouses, and that sort of thing. Even all this had been somewhat organized. The rest of the huge expanse was as trim as a barracks waiting for inspection. No dust was on the floor, no cobwebs hung from the rafters, and the windowpanes were clear. Somebody—Phyllis, at a guess—must have made sure that it got a going-over once or twice a year.

From the attic I went downstairs to the kitchen and made myself a cup of instant coffee, washing up afterward and replacing everything carefully. I made a fast pass through the kitchen cabinets and drawers, and then began to search the rest of the ground floor. I didn't expect to find anything of much significance in this relatively public part of the house, where guests and servants were most likely to go poking into things. And I didn't. The only partial exception was in the study off the living room, where Kellicott kept various souvenirs of his travels—the equivalent, at his level, of plaster Eiffel towers and Disneyland bumper stickers.

On the wall was a glass-fronted case that held a collection of brilliant, iridescent rain-forest butterflies, arranged by someone with such an eye for color and composition that they almost amounted to art. A small god or devil that looked pre-Columbian sat on a shelf, and a stylized pendant from the same period hung from a nearly invisible filament inside a hand-blown bell jar. Both seemed to be solid gold, although perhaps they weren't. It was hardly likely that Kellicott would set that much temptation in the path of the help, or of burglars like me, for that matter.

A miniature bayonet sat on Kellicott's green blotter. It was an exact duplicate in sterling silver of a U.S. Army bayonet, down to the saw teeth on the back of the blade and the blood gutter down its length. The silversmith had even fashioned tiny silver rivets to hold the silver grips on the haft. The whole letter opener or ornament or whatever was about ten inches long. "A Alden con amistad, Roberto, San Salvador, 1979" was engraved on the blade. With friendship, from Roberto.

Roberto D'Aubuisson, the psychopathic death squad commander? It seemed possible. Carter's foreign policy by the time of Kellicott's appointment, after many months of listening to Brzezinski's cold war puerilities, was edging away from human rights and toward Jeane Kirkpatrick's worldly-wise tolerance of torturers and murderers.

I also found a cheap bronze casting of the Liberty Bell on Kellicott's desk. The small plaque on the base said "To Alden Kellicott, U.S. State Department, from the City of Philadelphia, Frank Rizzo, Mayor." Presumably he kept this around as a joke; maybe he kept the bayonet as a joke, too. Or maybe he kept it because the silver knife was such an elegant toy.

So was the chrome-plated Beretta semiautomatic pistol I found in his desk drawer, or at least the Soldier of Fortune set would have considered it a toy. Its .25-caliber bullets would have very little of what the gun freaks call stopping power. On the other hand, the weapon of choice used by Mafia killers is the .22. And their victims wind up just as dead, clinically, as a man whose head has been exploded by a .357 Magnum. Kellicott's more modest pistol was a gift of state. According to the engraved inscription it came from a prominent West Point graduate who went on to success as the ruling kleptocrat of Nicaragua, the late Anastasio Somoza.

I grew up with long guns and still own two of them. But when I was in Southeast Asia I grew out of emotional puberty—at least the NRA's brand of it. I came to see that handguns were up to practically no good, and I have never since carried one. Nor do I much like the idea of other people having them available for use, and so I unloaded this one, replaced the clip, then slipped the smooth, heavy bullets into my pocket.

So far I had sifted through most of the house and had come up with a sieve full of nothing. Maybe Kellicott should have turned his gifts from foreign suitors over to the Department of State—it seemed to me that I had read something to that effect somewhere, someplace. But it wasn't the sort of thing that either Phil Jeffers or the Senate Foreign Relations Committee was likely to get too upset over.

What remained, though, was what I figured would be the most promising area—the upstairs living quarters. I started with Mrs. Kellicott's boudoir.

Her bedside drawers held a half dozen Harlequin

romances, squirreled away out of sight. Out of whose
sight? Her intellectual husband's? Apart from this,
though, all I learned from my search was that she hadn't
been lying about where she hid her booze. There was
an opened fifth of Jack Daniel's at the bottom of her
blanket chest.

In her bathroom the medicine cabinet held a jumble
of pill bottles, some of the prescriptions years out of
date and some of them recent. The prescriptions had
been written by ten or a dozen different doctors, the
sign of the pillhead. Some of the brand names I didn't
recognize, but many I did. Among them were Valium,
Inderal, Thorazine, Lithane—the pharmacology of the
emotionally frail. There was a minimum of cosmetics
and other toiletries, compared with the amazing excess
you find in most women's bathrooms. No male parapher-
nalia was in sight.

Kellicott's bedroom didn't contain much of interest,
either, except his Rolodex. I once heard someone accuse
Phil Jeffers of having an upwardly mobile Rolodex. Kellicott didn't. There was no more upward to go to. The
cards flapped down as I turned the little wheel: Henry,
Cy, Zbig, Brent, George (Kennan, Shultz, Baker, and
Bush), and on and on. I spent ten minutes copying down
the private, unlisted numbers of the rich and famous.
You never know when you might want to give the Ron
a ring.

The books on the shelves held nothing but evidence
that he had read most of them: underlinings and notes
in the margin. It took nearly an hour to riffle the pages
of each one, but books seemed like the best of places to
hide anything small that needed hiding. The second-
best place for written secrets was probably the oak filing
cabinets, particularly since they were locked. I found
the key hanging on a small finishing nail driven into the

side of a desk drawer, so far to the rear that you had to pull the drawer nearly free of its tracks to spot it. The files could have kept me happily occupied for days, but I didn't have days. I only had till evening, at the latest, and maybe not that long. Kellicott was due at work Monday morning; he would have to catch a Sunday ferry off the Vineyard and spend tonight at home in Cambridge. And so I had to be content with thumbing through each folder to make sure that it did indeed contain only "Personal correspondence, Jan.–July 1987" or whatever else the label said. And each folder did. "Miscellaneous" was even miscellaneous, although of no particular interest.

Next I went through Emily's room, or memorial. I wondered who had made the decision to leave all her belongings in place. Maybe, like a lot of decisions, it had just got made by inertia. Much of the gear of upper-class female adolescent life was there, but it said little about the owner. There was a tape deck, but no tapes that would have indicated her taste in music. Presumably she had taken them with her. I found no diaries, letters, marked calendars, engagement books, notes to herself, sketches. Probably she had taken all that, too. The only books were old schoolbooks, and the usual little-girl collection of Nancy Drew and books about horses. I had the feeling that the answer to Emily/Nelda's death was somewhere in her life—but her old room offered no answers that I could see.

Nothing to do but to continue rooting around like a blind hog, and so I went back to Phyllis's room to search it more fully, now that the sun had risen. Nothing under the throw rugs, and no sign that the maple floorboards had ever been tampered with. The closet and the bureau drawers contained nothing unexpected; nor did her bedside tables. In the bathroom, I found a supply of birth control pills tucked away in the back of one of the dressing table drawers. I was surprised, not that she would hide them, but that she would have them at all. I wouldn't have imagined that she had an active enough love life to justify being on the pill, and yet the date on the prescription was only a couple of months back. Good for you, Phyllis, I thought. Maybe you'll get out of this nut ward yet. I closed the drawer, and went back out to the bedroom to have a look at the writing desk.

The light was good enough by now to let me see clearly. The desk was the sort of thing you might see in a museum. It had a row of cubbyholes and tiny drawers above the shelf on which you wrote. The writing surface was of green Moroccan leather inlaid into mahogany. To the right of the kneehole were three good-sized drawers. The hardware on them had the soft shine and blurred edges that come from a couple centuries of polishing. In the top drawer I found ledgers, bankbooks, and bills sorted into envelopes or paper-clipped bundles.

Phyllis, it turned out, ran the house. Her name was printed on the checks along with her mother's and father's. To judge from the stubs, filled in carefully and legibly, she was in charge of paying the help, the insurance, the property taxes, and all other household bills. The largest single outlay was for the salaries and Social Security for Bridget and Otto, a gardener-houseman, and a full-time caretaker on the Vineyard. They even got their health insurance paid, which made Kellicott an unusually generous employer of domestic help. The family owned a Cherokee for use on the island, and three other cars, all Saabs of various ages. Heating oil, utilities, major and minor maintenance of the two residences, all were high. A thousand here, a thousand there, it all added up. Each month Phyllis got through most of the twenty thousand dollars deposited monthly into the Kellicotts' account by the Milton Family Trust. Very nearly a quarter of a million dollars a year. It cost more than I thought to be rich.

But it didn't cost Susan Kellicott any more to be a drunk than it had cost me in the old days. The purveyor to the Kellicotts was a liquor dealer of the old school, who sent handwritten, itemized bills monthly. Kellicott's spritzers accounted for about two bottles of his brand of white wine a week. The rest of the family also drank wine at dinner, or had when I was their guest. This seemed to account for about a bottle a day of what looked to be good stuff, although about the best I can do myself is tell white from red. I understood another regular purchase better: five fifths a week, week in and week out, of Jack Daniel's bourbon. That meant a habit of pretty close to a bottle a day, and I figured the eight bottles of sherry a month were probably Mrs. Kellicott's, too.

This only attached numbers to what I had already learned from Mrs. Kellicott, of course. What was new to me, though, was the thought of Phyllis sitting here at this beautiful antique desk, year after year, signing the bills for the slow poisoning of her mother. Was she worried about being an enabler, as they call people like her on the talk shows? Or did she just see her role in the process as part of the job Papa had handed her? What did she feel for her mother? Pity? Contempt? Nothing?

The bottom drawer of the desk was the deepest of the three, deep enough to serve as a file cabinet. The folders were labeled—auto insurance, roofing estimates, bills (paid), and so on. I began to work my way through them, pulling a couple of items from each to judge if the rest might be promising. They weren't, by and large. But inside the file marked "Appliances, guarantees &

instructions" I saw a large manila envelope. By a lucky chance, I took a look in it.

When I popped the envelope slightly open, I could see just the edge of the top picture. All that showed was a slice of dark blue, with perhaps three quarters of an inch of flesh tone near the bottom, and yet I knew what had to be on the rest of the sheet, and what the rest of the envelope had to hold. I can't say how I was so sure, what locked on to what else in my head and then on to a dozen more things. But it was like coming up with just the right letter in a crossword puzzle, the one that suddenly made sense of four or five fragments of vertical and horizontal nonsense. I pulled the whole sheaf out of the envelope.

The blue was a couch. The flesh tone was part of the ankle of a young girl, naked. The pink tips of her small breasts still had the bulbous look of early puberty. The man was spurting onto them. You couldn't see his face. The idea of these things is to not see his face, so that it can be the buyer's. The rest of the pictures in the stack were much the same, but with different girls and different men, different positions, different openings. They had evidently been culled from a considerable number of kiddie-porn magazines. A collection of all-time hits.

At the bottom of the stack was what appeared to be a blank sheet of paper, protected by a cheap transparent folder of the type that kids use to protect important homework. I turned it over and on the other side was a pencil sketch of a black man lying propped up on one elbow, his chin cupped in his palm. He was posed on a rumpled bed, facing the viewer. His upper leg was partly bent, the knee cocked in the air; his lower leg was slightly bent, too, but lay flat on the bed. His penis lay over his upper thigh, as if it had been slung to one side and abandoned. The sketch was a wonderful one, done with an assured minimum of lines, its subject suggested rather than insisted upon. The man was Pink Lloyd.

The sketch was unsigned, but of course I knew who the artist had been.

All of a sudden I had a lot of important calls to make. It was time to leave. Walking out of a house where you have no business being, in midday and in full view of the neighbors, is a scary thing to do. I had been thinking about it off and on since the break-in, and couldn't come up with any solution but to stride right out of the place as if I belonged there and hope for the best.

Initially I had thought of waving good-bye to an imaginary host, but in the end I abandoned the idea. Too cute. I just closed the front door behind me, walked with an entirely false confidence out the curving driveway, turned right on the street, and went to my car around the corner. As far as I could tell, nobody noticed a thing. That's the great, cruel lesson of the world, of course: most people out there aren't even watching when you make a fool, or a saint, of yourself. And if they were, most of them wouldn't understand what was in front of their eyes, or care if they did understand.

And so off I went, another criminal getting away scotfree while the police and honest burghers slept. On my way home, I pulled briefly and illegally into one of the parking spaces in front of the Weld boathouse so that I could toss the bullets from Kellicott's clip into the Charles. They disappeared immediately from view into water with the visibility of coffee and cream. Toward the bottom the water thickened up into blackish muck, into which Kellicott's bullets would settle and eventually become part of the earth's geological record. I headed for home, and my telephone.

10

LLOYD? LISTEN, LLOYD, THIS IS TOM BETHANY, THE GUY you talked to . . ."

"It's cool, I know who you are."

"Yeah, well, what it is, I need to know what happened to those pictures of you that Emily drew."

"Nelda."

"Nelda, right. She give you the pictures?"

"What I want them pictures for? I know what I look like."

"She kept them, then?"

"Far's I know. What you got, man?"

"Nothing, really. Not yet. I'm putting it together."

"You putting it together, you know it's not me."

"I knew that all along."

"Everybody knew that but the man. Man don't know shit. As usual."

"Probably as usual for Sergeant Harrigan, anyway. I

don't imagine he asked you what happened when you left the massage parlor, did he?"

"Didn't nothing happen. I just left."

"Out the front door?"

"Sure. If there's a back door, I don't know nothing about it."

"Nelda went down with you, right?"

"She come on down, yeah. Say good-bye, you know?"

"How? Shake hands, wave at you, kiss you? What?"

"She give me like a little peck on the cheek. You believe that shit?"

I could see what he meant. How many pecks on the cheek does a pimp get, after all? "Were you inside or outside?" I asked.

"When she done that? Inside, at the bottom of the steps. Then I went on out and she went back upstairs and that was the last I seen of her. Next thing I know, she's in the paper dead."

"So you were in that little kind of entryway, behind the glass door?"

"That's it."

"The light was on inside?"

"I guess. I didn't notice was it on, but I guess I'd remember was it off."

"So anybody outside could have seen you?"

"Sure. Wasn't no secret."

"No, probably not."

I didn't like to call Hope Edwards at home, for fear of getting her husband instead. There's a certain awkwardness about talking to a man when you're sleeping with his wife, particularly when he probably knows it. Even when he most likely doesn't care or is even glad about it, as in this case, there's still a certain awkwardness.

But it was Sunday, and home was where she'd be—and, sure enough, Martin was the one who answered.

"Hey, Tom," he said with every appearance of friendship, "how are you? Good, good. Listen, she's upstairs changing to go out. Hold on, I'll go tell her you're on the line."

Changing. I'd be up watching, but Martin would probably just holler through the door. That's what marriage does to you, no doubt, but it was more than that in his case. Or so Hope has told me; I've never discussed it with Martin and never will, never would. Plenty of things are better left unsaid.

Hope had been first in her Georgetown Law School class. Martin was second, by an insignificant fraction. The beautiful Hope, the handsome Martin, both brilliant with promise. They made the perfect couple when they were married in St. Albans two weeks after graduation. They had the perfect baby, Lisa, ten months later. And then a long pause and then the two boys, only a year apart, one born on September 26 and the other the following September 28. The boys doubled up and celebrated their birthdays on the same date, the twenty-seventh. It never particularly struck anybody but Martin and Hope that the joint birthday fell about nine months after New Year's, the only night of the year that Martin ever allowed himself to get drunk. That both nights happened to work in well with Hope's ovulation cycle was, of course, an accident. The New Year's after the second son's conception Martin got drunk again, but that time he didn't make love to his wife. He lay there like a board, almost catatonic, and told Hope it tore him apart but he had to leave her. She could have the house, the money, the children, everything. All he wanted was Louis, his partner in men's doubles.

Hope's first feeling was relief, that there was no other

woman. Next she knew that she didn't want him to leave the children. He was a wonderful father regardless of his sexuality—maybe even, now she thought of it, in some measure because of it. The children needed him to go on being their father, and he needed it nearly as much as they did. In the following days and weeks they worked out an agreement, the two of them, as much unspoken as spoken. He would have Louis, but never bring him into the life of the family. If she found someone, as he hoped she would, she would do the same.

Hope didn't even look for someone, though. She poured everything into her children and into her career. By 1980 she was on the domestic policy staff at the White House, and that fall she took leave to do advance work for Carter's reelection campaign. I was on the road, too, trying to keep the Secret Service and local officials from getting dangerously mad at each other. That began it for Hope and me. Since then we have stayed apart, and this is the plain truth of it, for the sake of the kids.

Now I heard the two boys hollering at each other over something important to them, and Hope telling them to keep it down, and then Hope on the line. "Tom," she said. "What's up? Can't talk, just taking the dwarfs off to the zoo."

And, in the background, "*Mommy, we're not dwarfs.*"

"Ask them how come they're so little, if they're not dwarfs."

"Can't, no time. Really. Our ride's waiting outside."

"Okay, quick. I need to know about the old rich. Who do you know that's old rich?"

"Plenty of people, from fund-raising. What do you need them for?"

"I need to talk to somebody with old money and smart enough so that he's thought about the people he grew up with."

"Somebody who leads the examined life, huh? Try Toby Ingersoll."

Her American Civil Liberties Union colleague, who had been Kellicott's aide, who wore dirty sneakers and socks with clocks on them. "Of course," I said. "Shit, I should have guessed it from his clothes."

"His town house is on Louisburg Square, but it's Sunday. Try him out at the family place in Manchester. I may have the number somewhere, but anyway it's probably listed. Old money has listed phones."

"I think I have the number already. Go to the zoo."

"I'm off. Call me later?"

I did have the number. It was one of the ones I had copied from Kellicott's Rolodex. Whoever answered went off to find Ingersoll, and I heard the deep barking of a dog. If the receiver had been more powerful, I imagine it would have picked up the sound of tennis balls being hit and the splashing at poolside and, off somewhere on the grounds, the steady growl of a power mower.

"Hi, Tom," Ingersoll said. "Good to hear from you."

"What kind of dog was that barking? A Great Dane?"

"A Lab, actually. Old now, but a wonderful dog in his day. He bit the head off a cairn terrier once."

"You're shitting me."

"No, it's true. Did you know J. Edgar Hoover used to keep cairns? That's true, too. Always had two of them. One of them called G-boy. Maybe that one was for his boyfriend, Clyde Tolson, that part I don't know. But I do know that every year he'd get District of Columbia dog tags number one and two for them. Was that what you called to find out?"

"No, I wanted to find out how rich people feel about poor boys who marry their daughters."

"Do you have our mutual friend in mind?"

"Yes."

"Then let's talk hypothetically, all right?"

"You're worried about the line?"

"Probably it's all right, but maybe it isn't. The present administration is opposed to civil rights, except for corporations."

"Hypothetically, then, what would a stupid bully with a pisspot full of money think about a poor but bright lad that married his daughter?"

"Hypothesizing that his daughter was pretty badly messed up, the old man would probably be grateful that he was able to hire her a faithful, presentable live-in nurse."

"What if he wasn't faithful? The nurse?"

"Be all right, probably. As long as he was careful, totally discreet. Or at least discreet enough so that no talk about it would get around."

"The point being not to hurt her?"

"The point being, a bargain's a bargain. I'm not talking about anything written down or spelled out here, but the old man would understand it wasn't a love match. He might have been stupid, but he wasn't blind. And very rich people live their whole lives in a state of constant suspicion that everybody else is trying to get their money away from them. Particularly everybody of the opposite sex. That's why they usually marry other rich people."

"And when they don't, they expect their money's worth?"

"Exactly right. Here's this little wounded birdie, you understand me, kind of dragging one wing through life. You pick her up and take care of her and they won't mind taking care of you. Long as you did as good a job as any man could reasonably be expected to, you could grow up to be secretary of the navy. Even a U.S. senator."

"Even secretary of state."

"Even that."

"But if you hurt her . . ."

"Oh, you could hurt her, maybe. What the hell, she's only a woman, and she was damaged goods at that. But you couldn't be *seen* to be hurting her. The minute you were, doors would start closing on you in certain places all over America."

"What places?"

"Bar Harbor, La Jolla, Manchester, Blue Hill, Shaker Heights, Sewickley Heights, Grosse Pointe, Red Bank. Those kinds of places."

"Would that matter? If your hypothetical ambition was to hold a very high government job?"

"Oh, it would matter."

"A lot?"

"A whole lot."

After I hung up I thought about bargains. Gladys Williams knew about bargains, too, only she called them balances. I thought about Hope and myself, and our bargain. And about Alden and Susan Kellicott with their separate domains up on the second floor, and their bargain. I thought about Emily, Nelda, whichever, and something hit me all at once. I wanted to call Hope with it, but she was at the zoo and so I called Gladys instead. She sounded a little odd, slightly out of breath.

"Is this a bad time to call?" I asked.

"Actually, yes," she said. "I'm just breaking in a new guy here."

"Shit, I'm sorry. I'll call later."

"No, go ahead."

"It's Nelda. Emily Kellicott's stage name, you know?"

"Sure, I know."

"It's one of those what-do-you-call-its. All I can think of is acronyms."

"Anagrams."

"Right. It's an anagram for Alden."

"No shit, Sherlock."

"You knew? Why didn't you tell me?"

"Never occurred to me you didn't know. It jumped right out at me, the minute you told me her father's name."

I hung up, trying to remember whether I had told Hope about the new name Emily had taken. If I had, probably it had jumped right out at her, too. You miss a lot, belonging to the slower sex. Plodding along, I called Wanda Vollmer and got a tinny version of her voice on a machine.

"You have reached Personal Leisure World," it said. "We can't come to the phone, but if you'll leave your name and number after the beep, we'll get back to you as soon as we can."

"Wanda," I said. "Listen, Tom Bethany. We were talking earlier about Nelda, okay? . . ."

"I'm here, Bethany," cut in Wanda, live. "What's up?"

"I thought of something I should have asked you before. The man who walked out on Nelda without getting a massage? The night she was killed?"

"Right."

"Did he ask for her by name?"

"No. I always ask do they want any special girl, you know, but he said it was his first time in the place."

"You've got that book with all the girls' pictures. Did he pick her out from her picture?"

"He didn't ask, so I didn't show him the book. Besides, she was the only one free."

"How did it work? Did Nelda come out?"

"She was still straightening up after the last customer.

I was busy, so I called her on the intercom to make sure she had fresh towels and stuff, then I told him go on back, number six."

"What did you say exactly? On the intercom, I mean?"

"Shit, Bethany, how can I remember? Probably something like, 'All set back there, Nellie? I got a customer for you.' "

"Nellie? *Nellie?*"

"I'd call her Nellie. It was like a pet name I had for her. A nickname, you know? There was this nun I had a crush on, I was eleven. Sister Nellie."

"A nun?"

"Don't you go getting no ideas now. I was the one had the crush, not her."

"You sure you called her Nellie instead of Nelda?"

"I'm positive."

"I was asking because you didn't seem exactly sure of what you said over the intercom."

"Nellie I'm sure of."

"Why?"

"Because she asked me that very same thing herself after the guy took off. Said she couldn't recall whether I called her Nellie or Nelda, and which was it? By the way, she asked me whether the guy had seen her picture, too. Same as you just asked me."

"How come she asked?"

"She said she was trying to figure out how come the guy took off like that."

"How would that help her figure it out?"

"I don't know."

I hung up feeling mildly pleased that there was at least one woman in this whole business who knew less than I did. Hoping that there would be another one, too, I dialed the Kellicotts' house on Martha's Vineyard. Phyllis Kellicott answered. She had a small, light, pleasant voice and a tentative way of speaking, as if she were constantly afraid of giving offense. From her voice, you'd picture the sort of girl who smiles apologetically when someone bumps into her.

"I'm afraid Papa's gone to the ferry," she said when I identified myself. "I could get Mummy."

"That's okay," I said. "You're the one I wanted to talk to."

"Me? Oh. All right."

"Quick question, that's all. Where were you the night Emily died?"

"Me? I was visiting friends on Hilton Head."

"South Carolina?"

"Yes. I got down there two weeks before Emily died, but Papa didn't call me till two days after. When they, you know . . ."

"Uh-huh." When they dug the body out of the snowbank. "How long were you down there?"

"It was going to be three weeks, but of course I flew right back. Are you sure you don't want to talk to Mummy?"

"No, no need to bother her."

Instead I dialed Markham for President headquarters, with the idea of bothering Phil Jeffers. He might very well be available for bothering, since campaigns don't shut down on Sundays. But he wasn't. To keep my skills sharp, I tried to con his home phone number out of the volunteer on the switchboard. But either they weren't sharp enough or she was.

"I'm sorry, Mr. Tiffany, but we're not permitted to give out home numbers," she kept saying until I figured it was no use going on.

"Well, have him call me as soon as he checks in. And it's not Tiffany. It's Bethany."

"*Bethany!* Why didn't you *say* so? He's been going

202

crazy trying to reach you. He's had me calling some Mr. Tasty or something for hours, only you're never in."

So she gave me Phil Jeffers's number, and I was able to bother him after all.

"Where the fuck you been?" he said. "I pay you a goddamn fortune, you don't even return my calls."

"Stop shouting, Phil. What is it, you think you look cute when you shout?"

"Listen to me, goddamn it . . ."

I hung up the phone, waited a few minutes, and called him back. This time he wasn't shouting. Jeffers was a pragmatist. If one approach didn't work, he'd try another.

"Jesus, don't hang up," he said. "I'm sorry I hollered. I been going crazy trying to get you, is all."

"Well, you got me."

"You said you were going to do some last-minute poking around, right? Kellicott? Nothing came up, am I right?"

"I'd hold off on him for now."

"Hold off?"

"Easy, Phil. I'm delicate."

"I can't hold off, for Christ's sake. Somebody leaked it to the *Globe*."

"Somebody."

"Well, you know how it goes."

"You shouldn't have done that, Phil. I was you, I'd unleak it."

"How can I fucking unleak it?"

"You can handle it. I read where you're the consummate political insider."

"Give me a break, Tom, will you? *Newsweek* calls me something, how can I help it what they call me?"

"Maybe you could demand a retraction."

"How the hell do I always get off the subject when

I'm talking to you, Tom? What's the problem with Kellicott?"

"Nothing, really. Weirdness, that's all."

"Shit, weirdness is in the job description. Look at Haig. Look at Kissinger."

"Look at Shultz."

"Shultz?"

"Sure. He had a tiger tattooed on his ass."

"So?"

"Don't you think that's weird, Phil?"

"Not particularly."

"Are you trying to tell me you've got a tiger tattooed on your ass, Phil?"

"Jesus, will you stop changing the subject? What about Kellicott? We're on Kellicott here."

"I just told you about Kellicott. In fact, I told you yesterday, and you went to the *Globe* anyway. Put up a little trial balloon, didn't you? You'd asked me yesterday, I'd have told you just what I'm telling you now. Call up the *Globe* and shoot down your little balloon."

"For Christ's sake, what new shit have you got?"

"No new shit I can prove yet! I'll tell you when I can! And Phil? Phil?"

"What?"

"You're shouting again."

And I hung up.

Through the long summer evening I sat in my La-Z-Boy recliner, thinking. The thinking was all right to do, here in Cambridge, but the La-Z-Boy wasn't. I'd be ruined if it got out that I'd rather be comfortable in an ugly recliner than uncomfortable in an ugly Eames chair.

What I was thinking about was my hypothesis. I was holding it up every way I could against the facts, to see how it matched up with them. Sure enough, it did. It was the simplest hypothesis that could explain all the

facts, so that I was on solid ground as far as Occam's razor goes. In Cambridge everybody knows what Occam's razor is, although there is some dispute over whether to spell it Occam or Ockham. If I could answer that one in 450 pages or less, they'd give me tenure at Harvard and I could spend the rest of my life in the faculty club dribbling oatmeal down the front of my cardigan.

As it was, I was doing a pretty neat job of getting a bottle of Sam Adams down me without spilling, in a La-Z-Boy recliner. And what was bothering me about Occam's razor was that while my hypothesis explained all the facts just fine, I didn't have enough facts to impress even myself. Where's the evidence, Judge Wapner would say, and I'd just be standing there like a retard. The Wapper's a lot tougher on evidence than they are at the faculty club.

Every twenty minutes or so I hit the redial button and called Kellicott's answering machine again, just on the off chance he somehow wasn't still stalled in the traffic jam that ran from Cape Cod to Boston on hot Sundays in August. It was 9:30, and dark, before Kellicott picked up. Pitching my voice high I asked for Martina, but was told I must have the wrong number. I grabbed my car keys off the top of the dresser.

11

I PARKED RIGHT IN KELLICOTT'S DRIVEWAY, INSTEAD OF around the block as I had the night before. His downstairs lights were on. He must have spotted me coming into the drive, since he opened the door almost before the bell had stopped ringing. "Tom!" he said. He didn't break into a broad, welcoming smile, but his face and his voice made it plain that I was just the person he had been waiting for all evening. "Listen, come on in. I was just getting myself some iced tea. Can I get you some? Or something else?"

Why not? We were both civilized people, after all. "Sure," I said. "Iced tea would be fine." He sat me down in the study to wait while he went for the tea.

"What can I do for you?" Kellicott said when we were both settled down in our chairs, comfortably sipping.

"I've just about got this business wrapped up," I said. "One or two more things, and I should be able to turn a preliminary report over to Jeffers tomorrow."

"Fine."

"I talked to Phyllis today."

"Phyllis? She's on the Vineyard."

"That's where she was, all right. I used the phone."

The sudden mention of Phyllis had kicked him slightly off the rails; Kellicott ordinarily was a step or two in front of a conversation, and not behind it as he had just seemed to be.

"She said she had been down on Hilton Head for a couple weeks before Emily got killed," I went on. "Must be tough on you when she's away."

"Tough on me?" He sounded puzzled, mildly curious. Now he was back on top of things.

"Doesn't she run the house normally?"

"Yes, she does. Damned well, too, although she wouldn't have mentioned that to you. Phyllis tends to keep her light pretty much under a bushel."

"I'll bet she does."

Kellicott looked at me for a moment before he answered. "This conversation is getting a little strange," he said. The conversation would have seemed even stranger, of course, if he had pretended not to notice my odd remark. Maybe he *was* the right man to sit on our side of the negotiating table at Geneva, after all.

Just then the phone rang. Kellicott made no effort to get it, and so we both just sat there listening as his recorded voice invited the caller to leave a message after the beep. And after the beep, as we both continued to sit there, came the voice of Phil Jeffers.

"Alden, we've got some kind of trouble," Jeffers said. "My guy Bethany says we should hold off till he talks to me tomorrow and for Christ's sake we slipped it to the *Globe* already. Call me as quick as you get in, I'm home all night."

We heard the click as Jeffers hung up.

"All right," Kellicott said, "what's this all about?" The easy charm was gone, utterly.

"What he said. I told him to sit on any announcement till I had a chance to clear some things up."

"What things?" It might have been Kellicott's father-in-law, laying into Kellicott's father after the town car ran out of gas on the way to the airport. I figured I wasn't going to be head of security for the State Department anymore, so what the hell . . .

"I'll tell you what things. You murdered your daughter and fucked her after she was dead."

Kellicott was silent for a moment that got long very quickly. When he spoke, the icy anger was gone. He sounded sad.

"Is that what you think?" he said. "You couldn't have any children. No one with children could say a thing like that."

I let that go. "For a long time I couldn't figure out why she was naked," I said.

Kellicott remained silent. A tiny shake of the head, almost imperceptible, suggested disagreement, or disbelief, or amazement, or who knows what.

"Think of all the things that don't fit," I went on. "It's a cold, raw night. Cars are going by on Lowell, near enough so that you'd be seen if you were crazy enough to take off your clothes and lie down in a snowbank to get laid. You wanted to get laid, you'd get in a car to do it, wouldn't you? What do you think, Alden?"

I figured this was the time to take him up on his invitation to call him by his first name.

Kellicott said nothing.

"Of course it couldn't have been her own car," I went on. "If it had happened in her car, the killer would have just left her in it. Why haul her out, stick her in a snowbank, lock her car back up, stick the keys in her purse, and stick the purse in the snowbank, too?

"Suppose it happened in the killer's car, though? Then it would make pretty good sense to shove her and her things into the nearest snowbank. Wouldn't that make sense, Alden?"

Kellicott made no answer. Get it out of your system, his mild expression said.

"Only why would she have gotten into a stranger's car, though? Force? He showed her his knife, maybe? A possibility. But not a probability, once I got to know a little about your daughter. She wasn't scared of much of anything, was she? Certainly not of her papa. Did she call you Papa? No, she didn't, did she? That was the whole trouble."

Kellicott kept on waiting for this lunatic to get tired and run down.

"Pink Lloyd's car was around earlier, of course. Maybe it was his car she got into, the way Sergeant Harrigan thinks. But why would Pink Lloyd have carved his initials into her? Harrigan probably thinks he was just leaving his mark, like a punk kid with a spray can. You probably hoped somebody like Harrigan would wander along, somebody dumb enough to think that. And of course you were right. But Pink Lloyd isn't dumb enough to do that, which is the real point. I've talked to him, and I know.

"I also know he loved her, and that he loved her because she didn't love him. And that even if she decided to throw him a mercy fuck, she wouldn't have done it naked in his car on a freezing night. And I know you were waiting in the parking lot when Emily came down to the lighted entryway and kissed Pink Lloyd good night. So that's what happened, Alden. He drove off, you hung around till she got off work, and then you got her into your car."

I took a swallow of my iced tea. Kellicott didn't touch his.

"You asked her who the guy was and she told you. That's how you knew what initials to leave on her later. How does that feel, Alden? To slice into your own daughter's dead body? A lot of people would feel a little odd about that. No? Nothing, huh? Just like cleaning fish?"

He wouldn't be provoked. I went on.

"What the hell," I said, "no harder than strangling her, I guess. Once she stopped wriggling, there was nothing to keep you from taking her clothes off and having a look at last, was there? So you did it. Nothing to keep you from fucking her, either, so you did that too. That's what you big shots do, isn't it? Whatever you fucking feel like doing?"

Now I was getting provoked, but it was okay. No need to hold back. The dumber he thought I was, the better.

"How does it work after they're dead, Papa? I mean, wasn't she kind of . . . dry?"

"This isn't really you," Kellicott said. There was no anger in his voice—just pity, and understanding. All the anger was on my side. I had gotten to like Emily, to like her a lot.

"It isn't dry with Phyllis, is it?" I said. And that got to him, to the extent of a tiny flicker of his eyelids. "The two of you look at that kiddie porn together, don't you? Does that get her nice and wet for Papa?"

"You're disgusting, Bethany."

"No, I'm not. The one who did it is the one who's disgusting, Alden. Remember how disgusting Emily thought you were when you tried it out on her in the motel, on the way back from summer camp? Did she go to her mother for help? I wondered about that. My guess is she did, but you just conned or browbeat your sick, pathetic wife the way you always have. Then you started on poor little Phyllis as soon as she got old enough.

"Poor little Phyllis has been your real wife for years, hasn't she? That's why she is on the pill and your wife's on tranquilizers. That's why the bidet is in your bathroom and not your wife's. All you need from your wife is the money and the family influence. Phyllis is the one who runs the house and takes care of her poor papa's special needs."

"I can't imagine who's feeding you all this craziness, Bethany . . ."

"Sure you can. How could I know all this shit unless I broke into your house last night and searched it?"

"That's a crime."

"Get a grip on reality, Alden. Of course it's a crime. What are you going to do? File a goddamned complaint?"

"I might very well," he said, and smiled. "If I could find evidence, that is. Which I very much doubt. And evidence is crucial in these matters, isn't it?"

"Meaning I don't have any evidence, either?"

Kellicott got to his feet and began to move restlessly around the room. He stopped by the desk and rested one haunch on it. He could have reached the Beretta before I could reach him, and I hoped he would try. He didn't know it was empty, and the attempt would make me absolutely certain that I had figured things out correctly. But he picked up the little silver bayonet instead. That didn't worry me, either. There are a dozen ways of taking a knife off a man and all of them, in a mismatch like this one, would be virtually risk-free from my point of view. Kellicott put down the miniature bayonet as absently as he had picked it up. He crossed to the window and looked out into the night.

"You can't possibly have any evidence," he said, "because I didn't kill Emily."

"If you mean physical evidence, you're right," I said. "But I've got plenty of circumstantial evidence. You're dead, Alden. You just don't know it. Let me lay it out for you."

"Yes, why don't you do that."

"You're a special customer at a porno bookstore in the Zone. The kind you buy is kiddie porn, just about the only kind that's illegal. Lou at the store can identify you. And all this daddy–daughter shit winds up in Phyllis's bedroom.

"You're saying so what, I'll dump those dirty books as soon as this asshole leaves, and Phyllis will never talk. Well, maybe she won't and maybe she will. For example, supposing she finds out that as soon as she took off for a few weeks in South Carolina, you took off to the massage parlors to get your ashes hauled by other women? That was the part that took me the longest to figure out. Right up till today I was working on the assumption that you went to Personal Leisure World to see Emily. But you didn't have any idea she worked there till you walked in with a hard-on, did you? Must have been an interesting couple of minutes, once you both got over your surprise.

"So out you go, wondering what to do next. You've got a certain problem here. A man sneaking off to a massage parlor and stumbling on to his own daughter, now that's news. Anything that weird, the whole goddamned *Social Register* would hear about it as soon as Emily opened her mouth in the right places. And she would, too. Maybe the frightened thirteen-year-old kid didn't know who to talk to, but the grown-up woman did. You have to talk to her, find out what she's got in mind.

"So you wait in your car. You see her saying good-bye to some black guy, and then you wait again till she gets off work. You call out to her and she gets into your car. Why not? It's cold, and she's not scared of you. She started standing up to you when she was thirteen. Who's your black friend, you ask her, and she tells you. Again, why not?

"My guess is you tried to tell her you heard she was working at Personal Leisure World, and you came looking for her the way you had before. Bullshit to that, she says. I checked with the manager and you didn't even know my name before you walked through that door.

"Who knows why you strangled her? To keep your rich pals from dumping you? Because you tried to screw her and she wouldn't let you this time either? Because you're a sociopath and it just seemed like a good idea at the time?

"Anyway, you do it, and then, what the hell, let's strip her and have a look. When you showed up at the Top Hat she ran you off before you could check her out, didn't she? Nothing she can do about it now, though. Long as she's bare-ass, well, what the hell, might as well spit on your dick and throw a fuck in her, right?"

His eyelids flickered once more.

"Why, you son of a bitch," I said. "That's just what you did, isn't it? You spat on it."

Nothing more showed. He had iced up again, but I knew I was right.

"When you're done you carve Pink Lloyd's initials on her to confuse the cops. What if I come over and look through your pockets, Alden? Will I find a knife of some kind there? A lot of men carry a sharp little penknife. Do you want me to come over?"

"As a matter of fact, I do carry a penknife."

"Let me have it."

"Don't be absurd."

213

"Oh, shit," I said. "All right." I got to my feet, but Kellicott produced the penknife before I had to take it off him. I put it in my pocket.

"Maybe there's some blood on it you missed," I said. "Though I doubt it, after all this time."

"You probably carry a penknife yourself," he said.

"I do, only I use mine for nails, not tits. Anyway, Sergeant Harrigan turns out to be dumb enough to think Emily was one of Pink Lloyd's whores and he killed her for some pimp reason. So everything is fine for a couple of years until this prick Bethany shows up and starts asking questions about you in dirty bookstores. Did you hear about that from Lou at the bookstore, or from Phil Jeffers? Doesn't matter. The point is, I was looking around in the part of your life that led straight to Emily's murder.

"Next thing I know this Jose Soto tries to knife me in the back. He worked as a volunteer for one of those do-gooder agencies in the basement of Old Cambridge Baptist. I figured he was an FBI plant, so for a long time I didn't make any connection between you and him. Not till I saw the toy bayonet you got from your death-squad buddy. Then I realized he probably wasn't an FBI plant at all, was he? He was a CIA plant from El Salvador. You probably knew him from the old days, when he was castrating peasants for your pal Roberto.

"Remember I mentioned Soto's name to you right afterward, asked you if you knew him? Of course you remember. It's why you killed him. You figured I'd eventually find him, since I knew his name. Maybe you even figured he told me his name, but he didn't. He was a tough little shit. I'm surprised you were able to dump him off the bridge, even with his bad arm. I suppose he trusted you, though."

Kellicott was still half standing, and half sitting on

214

the desk. In his shoes, I would have done the same thing he was doing: keeping quiet to find out what I had on him. So I went on telling him, because I wanted him to know that I didn't really have anything on him. Except for one thing, which I was just getting to.

"What you're thinking, Alden, is that all I've got here is a handful of air, and when I open my hand up there's nothing. Well, that would be true if it wasn't for Wanda Vollmer. Does the name mean anything to you?"

"I'm afraid I don't know Miss Vollmer, no. I don't know Mr. Soto, either, or Mr. Lloyd, or any of your other interesting friends."

"You'd recognize Miss Vollmer's picture, Alden."

"I very much doubt it."

"She recognized yours when I showed it to her," I lied. "She's the manager who took your money at Personal Leisure World."

"Really? I find that . . ."

And Kellicott caught me with a trick I had used dozens of times myself, to cut off an unwanted telephone call without seeming rude. You catch your caller off base by hanging up in the middle of your own line—hanging up, in effect, on yourself. Every time he'll blame the connection, not you.

Kellicott worked it so well on me that he managed to grab his gun and make it out the door of the study before I started to make sense. When I got to the door myself, he was disappearing around a corner. When I got to the corner, he was disappearing into a door next to the kitchen. When I got to that door, it turned out to lead into a pantry, and he was just slamming shut another door, at the far end of it. When I got to the other door, it was locked and he was slamming shut the first door. He had doubled back and locked me inside the dark pantry.

215

I knew how to handle that problem, having seen it done in scores of movies. I took a short run and smashed my shoulder into the door. It was like hitting heavy planking. So I made my way in the dark to the other end of the pantry, kneading my shoulder and hoping it wouldn't stiffen up too badly. But the other door seemed just as solid, when I tried it with my uninjured shoulder. I groped around till I found the light switch, and examined the situation. The door panels seemed to be the only possible point of attack. An old-fashioned soda-acid fire extinguisher made of brightly polished copper hung on the wall. I unhooked it to use as a battering ram on one of the door panels. Finally I was able to make a big enough opening so that I could reach through and unlock the pantry door from outside. By then Kellicott was gone, of course, and so was the car that had been parked in the driveway.

My plan had been to provoke him into making a run at Wanda, all right—but not until after the massage parlor's 10 P.M. closing. By then she would be safely away. I had figured on leaving Kellicott's house first, so that I would get to the massage parlor parking lot before him. When he showed, I would know for certain that he had killed his daughter, and probably Jose Soto as well. Then I could point the police at Wanda, and she would identify him. Once they knew for sure where to look, they wouldn't have much trouble putting together a case.

That was the plan.

But now Kellicott might be waiting when Wanda left. With her dead, the police could never make a solid case against him. It would only be my word that he had killed Wanda or anybody else. He would never be secretary of state, but he wouldn't spend the rest of his life in Walpole, either.

My first thought was to call Personal Leisure World

and warn Wanda, but all I got was the recorded message. Then I dialed 911 and it was already ringing before I thought the thing through and hung up. Even if I were able to fight my way up through the bureaucracy over the telephone and eventually get somebody in a position of responsibility, what would happen? A stranger calls with an improbable story about another stranger maybe on his way to a massage parlor, maybe with the idea of murdering someone who may have seen him shortly before a crime he might have committed? I tried Personal Leisure World once again and got the answering machine once again before I ran for my car.

When I slowed down as I passed the little shopping center on Lowell Parkway, I was glad I hadn't made a fool of myself over the phone with the police. Everything seemed quiet. I couldn't see any lights on the second floor of the building where the massage parlor was, but then I didn't know whether any of its windows were on the street side anyway. The light in the downstairs entry was on, but it probably stayed on all night. Kellicott's Saab wasn't among the dozen or so cars parked in the lot, but I was still uneasy. He could have parked in the vast anonymity of the bigger and newer mall just across Lowell. Or he might not have arrived yet, in which case the mall sounded like a good idea for me, too. Since I had been parked alongside him in his driveway, he knew my car as well as I knew his. If I parked outside the massage parlor, I might scare him off. I turned into the big mall across the parkway, and walked back to the little shopping center.

I nearly got there too late.

Wanda Vollmer appeared in the lighted entryway, probably thirty yards from me. She locked the door to the stairway, locked the glass door from the outside,

217

replaced the keys in her purse, and headed toward her car. I began to head the same way, but stopped when a man rose up from between two cars. "Wanda Vollmer?" Kellicott said, just loud enough so that I could make out the words.

"Who wants to know?" Wanda demanded, much louder. Wanda took minimum shit off men.

Since her answer was in effect a yes, Kellicott moved instantly. He moved in too close for her to knee or kick effectively, grabbed her throat with both hands, and set out to strangle her.

"Hey," I shouted, and started to run. Kellicott pushed Wanda away and turned toward me, tugging at something in his pocket. The Beretta finally came free. As I charged, he leveled the unloaded gun at me, aimed it carefully—and it fired. The bullet felt like a sharp, hard punch to the left side of my chest. I stopped two or three steps short of Kellicott, more from surprise than from the impact.

Movement from Wanda, and a sound.

Kellicott was on the ground howling, his hands to his eyes. He was twisting around in agony, like a just-hooked worm. Wanda was holding something in her hand. She bent over and jammed the thing into Kellicott's face and it made the hissing sound again, like an aerosol bomb. He screamed louder and rolled away, leaving the gun forgotten on the pavement. I bent to pick it up.

"Holy shit," I said. "What did you do to him?"

"Mace, the fucker. I always wondered if it worked."

"You know who he is?"

She looked at him closely, the best she could with him twisting around and covering his eyes.

"No," she said. "Yes? Maybe if I could see him better. He could be the guy who came in . . ."

"That's right. Nelda's father."

"Nelda's fucking *father!*"

"Exactly."

"Shit, that's blood on you," Wanda said.

"I don't think it's too bad."

"What are you, a doctor?"

"I was shot once before, and it felt a lot worse."

"Yeah, well, you better come inside and let me have a look." She remembered Kellicott. "By the way, what are we going to do with fuckface?"

"Take him along."

She grabbed hold of one foot with her two good arms, and I got the other with my one good arm, and we dragged him toward the building. He was too busy trying to breathe and dealing with the agony in his eyes to fight back. As we hauled him up the flight of concrete steps his head smacked into each one like a cantaloupe hitting the floor, and after a couple of times he stopped wriggling. He was still unconscious, which was probably a mercy, when we lugged him into the sauna.

"Now let's see what you got," she said, unbuttoning my sports shirt. When she had washed off the blood—very little blood, considering—I could see a small puncture wound with puffy lips and dark red center, already coagulating. The bullet had gone in just below my left nipple, perhaps two inches off to the side. "I'll be a son of a bitch, here it is," said Wanda, fingering my back right under the shoulder blade.

I managed to reach around with my good hand to feel for myself. The bullet made a round lump just under the flesh. I had felt the same thing before once, in the arm of an old Meo woman who had got in the way of one of Kissinger's antipersonnel bombs. She had laughed when she had me feel the steel ball bearing in her. Primitive sense of humor. Kissinger would have liked her.

The shock was wearing off and the pain was starting, a dull and constant bone ache. At least there wasn't the sharp, bright, stabbing pain of a broken rib when I breathed, though. My guess was that the little bullet had found its way between two ribs, and out between two more. Now it was lodged in the meat of my latissimus dorsi muscle.

"We better get you to a hospital," Wanda said.

"The hell with that," I said. "They might keep me there. Let me use your phone, okay?"

"Okay," she said, taking me over to it. "Listen, are you sure it was her *father* that killed Nelda? Because the guy that killed her, didn't he fuck her, too?"

"That's right, and he was her father. And he fucked her after she was dead. He came after you because you're the only one that saw him here that night."

She thought that over as I phoned Gladys Williams. "Is your friend still there?" I asked when she answered.

"Hey, what do you care? You'd call anyway. As a matter of fact, though, he's gone."

"Can you cut a bullet out of me? It's right under the skin."

"Can you drive?"

"Oh, sure."

"Come on over, then. I'll take a look."

And that was it. No hesitation, no questions. I would have fallen in love on the spot, if it hadn't been for Hope.

"What do I do with fuckface here?" Wanda said when I hung up. "Call the cops?"

"Not till I figure out what to tell them. You got a closet we can lock him into till I get back?"

"None of them lock. The sauna, maybe. I could jam the door shut with a mop handle."

She dragged his dead weight in there by herself, my left side having stiffened up. "I guess we should tie him up in case he comes to," she said. "Only what the fuck with?" She thought it over and said, "Dental floss."

"*Dental floss?*"

"One of the girls used to have a john who had her tie him up with it. Three or four rounds and nobody can break it. Cuts in too much when you pull against it." She went for her purse and brought out a plastic container. "This is the heavy-duty stuff," she said. "The tape."

It hurt, but I helped her hoist Kellicott into a semi-sitting position on one of the benches. She explained her idea as she worked Kellicott's pants and underpants off him. Then she looped the dental floss a half dozen times around one of the cedar planks in the bench. Next she looped a triple thickness of the tape around and around his scrotum. Not tight enough to hurt, but too tight for his testicles to pass through. Kellicott was making noises now, regaining partial consciousness. He wasn't back to the point, though, where he could do anything to stop Wanda from binding his thumbs together behind him with the floss so that he couldn't use his hands to free his scrotum.

"Let's see fuckface get loose now," she said when she had finished.

Back outside, she turned the heat down to zero and wedged her mop handle between the opposite wall and the sauna so that its door couldn't be opened from inside. "Just in case," she said, although in case of what, I couldn't imagine. The man was never born who would even have tried to yank himself out of that kind of noose. I looked through the small glass window at Kellicott. He was recovered enough so that he was rolling his head around, probably hoping he could ease the pain from his streaming eyes. I didn't know how long it took for the effects of Mace to wear off, and I didn't much care.

"I got to thank you," Wanda said. "It took a lot of balls to charge that gun."

"Actually, it didn't," I said. "I thought the son of a bitch was empty. Which reminds me." I pulled out the Beretta and removed the clip. It was indeed empty. I just hadn't thought to check and make sure there wasn't a round in the chamber. Somehow there was no consolation in the thought that I'd never make that mistake again. It was the kind of situation that was unlikely to come up twice, and so my lifetime stats were pretty sure to remain at 0 for 1.

I left things in Wanda's more-than-capable hands and set out for Gladys's place.

Gladys took me right to the bathroom, where I looked unenthusiastically at the tools laid out on a cloth bundle that she had unrolled on the top of her toilet tank.

"Why would you keep scalpels around?" I asked.

"Salesmen's samples. I've got lots of stuff. I could take your leg off, if I had to."

"I didn't ask where you got them, Gladys. I asked how come you had them around the house."

"To practice medicine. Hey, how else are you going to learn? Okay, now reach over and grab your far knee, that's it. Need to stretch the skin so I can see that lump . . ."

I felt her fingers exploring it, and then a hard, quick pressure, and then a lighter pressure from some wet pad or cloth that I assumed she was using to sterilize the area.

"Come on, get it over with," I said.

"It is over with." She began to wash something under the tap. "Popped out just like a big blackhead."

"You got a nice way of putting it, all right. Let's have a look."

She showed me the little slug, which was only slightly deformed. "My guess is it traveled around the inside of the rib cage for a few inches and then came out between two of them," she said. "If you had regular lats instead of those big goddamn slabs of muscle, it probably would have gone right on through."

"How come you didn't pass that blade through a flame before you sliced into me?"

"Not necessary. None of my patients ever get infected."

"Shit, Gladys, they're dead."

"I never think of them that way. I think of them like they were, well . . . my friends."

And so we chattered away, carefree as birds, while she put a couple of stitches into the cut and bandaged it over. She let me have the bullet and I slipped it into my pocket. Maybe I could get it bronzed. One way and another a good deal of time passed before I started to focus on the problem of what to do about Kellicott.

"Remember the detective lieutenant I told you about?" Gladys asked. "Curtin?"

"The smart one?"

"Yeah, well, you could be in pretty deep shit unless we get hold of a smart one."

"You figure Detective Sergeant Ray Harrigan might not really grasp what we've got here?"

"Might not, no. Why don't I call Billy Curtin instead, tell him we'll meet him at the massage parlor?"

"Where do you get this 'we' shit, white woman?"

"You think I'm missing this? Either it's 'we' or I don't call Curtin."

And so Gladys was with me when I returned to Personal Leisure World. Nothing that looked like a police car was in the parking lot, and so I assumed that Lieutenant Curtin hadn't shown up yet. We rang the night buzzer, and in a minute Wanda Vollmer came down to let us in.

"This is Gladys Williams," I said. "She just cut the bullet out of my back."

"Pleased to meet you, Doctor," Wanda said.

"Gladys is okay," Gladys said modestly.

"Maybe you should have a look at this guy we got," Wanda said. "He's not looking too good. Actually, I think maybe he's dead."

"Oh, shit, Wanda," I said.

"Hey, I didn't do nothing. Probably he had a bad heart. Some people can't stand the heat."

"Wanda, you turned the heat off. I saw you do it." I sounded stupid even to myself, and so I dropped it. "Oh, *shit*, Wanda," I said again.

"Hey, listen, he fucked her after she was dead, didn't he?"

"Probably."

"His own daughter. What could I do?"

Wanda shrugged, smiling. No doubt it was her normal smile, but it looked terrible to me. If Kellicott was really dead, that smile, through the little glass window of the sauna, was likely the last thing he ever saw.

"He's dead, all right," Gladys said after letting Kellicott's limp forearm, wrist, and hand flop back down on the cedar bench. "No pulse at all."

I had turned the heat off before we went into the sauna, and had left the door standing open. But it was still unbearably hot. Kellicott, naked from the waist down, sat in a puddle of sweat. His wet hair was plastered to his head. His sweat-soaked shirt was stuck to his body. I was starting to sweat myself, and so I went out to join Wanda at the doorway. Gladys, though, stayed inside. She examined the noose around Kellicott's scrotum, and then stuck her head under the bench to see exactly how he was attached to it.

"Pretty neat," she said. "No way he could have gotten to the knot."

She came out from the heat and wiped her face with her hand. "He'd of had to leave his balls behind to get out of that."

That made me think of something. "Where's the broomstick you jammed the door with, Wanda?" I asked.

"Back in the closet. What did I need with the broomstick? I still had my Mace."

I considered that.

"You showed him the door was open, didn't you? And then you cranked up the heat and looked through the window at him, didn't you? You *wanted* the son of a bitch to go for you."

Wanda looked pleased with herself, a big girl who had been caught by the nuns but wasn't at all ashamed of the bad actions she had committed.

"Well, it wasn't that so much," she said. "It was just I needed the door open so I could throw water on the rocks."

The thermometer had been at 102 degrees centigrade when Gladys and I went in, just above boiling. The human body can take it for a certain time at that temperature, but only if the humidity is so low that the evaporation of sweat can cool the system down. Tossing water onto the hot rocks has no effect on a wall thermometer, but it has an immediate effect on the human body. The sudden humidity slows down evaporation. From one second to the next, overheated but bearable air becomes scalding, suffocating.

"Jesus, Wanda," I said, "what are we going to tell the cops?"

The downstairs buzzer rang. "Shit," I said. "I guess we won't have time to work anything out. Well, we'll try the truth, or part of it anyway."

Lieutenant Curtin, the deputy chief of detectives, was with a uniformed sergeant who seemed not to have the power of speech, at least around Curtin. And Curtin was an intimidating man, although for no particular reason that met the eye. He was of short-medium height and physically unimpressive. In Laos I had known a small, scrawny case officer named O'Malley who could out-walk even the Meo born in those mountains. His last walk, before the CIA retired him on disability, was sixty kilometers through Pathet Lao territory after his Porter Pilatus was shot down. He had a bullet through one ankle and burns over most of the lower half of his body, but he made it out in nine days with no food. Lieutenant Curtin was the same kind of scrawny.

He looked in through the doorway at the body, a long look. He went inside and looked some more, at one point getting down the way Gladys had, to check on exactly how Kellicott's scrotum had been attached to the bench. He came out again and jerked his chin in my direction.

"This the guy you told me about?" he said to Gladys. He even sounded a little like O'Malley. Gladys nodded. "Okay," Curtin said to me. "Tell me about it."

"Can we do it alone?" I asked.

"The guy's okay, huh?" Curtin said to Gladys, and she nodded again. "Bethany, is that it? Okay, Bethany, let's go."

He led the way down the hall, never bothering to ask

if he could use a room, or which room. He opened the
first door he came to, and we went into one of the massage cubicles. For ten minutes, I told him about it. Like
me, he only fully bought it at the very end, when Kellicott began to strangle Wanda the instant he was sure
who she was.

"She'll testify to this, will she?" he asked.

"Oh, sure. So will I."

"It was pretty hot in there." The lieutenant gestured
again with his chin, in the general direction of the sauna
down the hall.

"She turned the heat off when we put him in there,"
I said. "I saw her."

"I guess those rooms hold the heat for quite a while,
don't they?"

"Yeah, I think you're right, Lieutenant."

"We got three things here, Bethany," he said. "First
we got the murder of this girl, this Emily, plus second
we got the guy in the river. On those murders we got
no evidence at all. Two open cases. Unsolved."

"Right."

"This thing we got here is the accidental death of this
girl's father. My guess is the guy's got it into his head
that the massage parlor was responsible somehow for
his daughter's death. With the grief, the brooding? Who
knows what ideas people get? Lucky for the manager
you happened by to save her life. Lucky for you the guy
completely missed you with this." He held up the little
Beretta I had given him.

"I know what you mean," I said, and I did. There was
a law saying that nondoctors—police lab technicians, for
instance—couldn't perform surgery without a license,
particularly on gunshot wounds.

"The sergeant and I are going downstairs to radio for

an ambulance," he said. "It'll take us a little while, you follow me?"

I thought about what we'd have to do: cut Kellicott loose, wrestle his underpants and pants and socks and shoes back onto him, get the mop handle back out to lock him in, get our stories straight.

"Think it'll take you ten minutes?" I asked.

"Probably about that."

"What about the autopsy, though?"

"We got this pathologist, he's kind of an elderly gentleman. He delegates, you know? To one of our people with a background in pathology. About all the old guy himself does these days, he signs the autopsy report she puts in front of him."

"She?"

"Right. It's a young lady."

"Probably she'll find out that Kellicott's system was under a lot of stress. All the excitement. Mace and everything."

"Yeah, I imagine," the lieutenant said. "What it'll probably be, she'll probably find out the guy had a weak heart or something."

"You don't mind my asking," I said. "Why are you doing this for her?" I didn't have to explain that I meant for Wanda, not for Gladys. Right from the beginning of my talk with Curtin it had been plain that there was no need to fill in the lines between the dots. We both saw the same picture.

"I was talking one time with the warden out at Framingham," Curtin said. "The women's prison, you know? From what the warden said, mostly you got your usual morons in there. Whores, thieves, addicts, like that. The place would have been a nightmare to administer except for the murderers."

"The murderers?"

"Yeah, the murderers ran the office, the switchboard, the library, the infirmary, kept all the books, everything. Smart, decent, responsible. Worked hard. You know who they had killed, most of them?"

"Their husbands?"

"You got it. Some prick that'd been kicking the shit out of them and the kids for ten, fifteen years."

"No loss, a guy like that," I said.

"No loss," Curtin agreed. "Those women, maybe they were technically murderers, but you still hated to see them spending the rest of their lives in jail. I'm speaking generally here, of course. After all, the law's the law, am I right?"

"Oh, absolutely."

"Well, we're out of here, Bethany," said Billy Curtin. "See you in ten minutes or so."

Actually it turned out to be a little more than ten minutes till Curtin came back upstairs with full reinforcements. Closer to fifteen minutes, really. Plenty of time to get the distinguished Phillips Professor of Political Economy ready for company.

I even would have had time to call Phil Jeffers, but I didn't do it. My weekly check from the campaign was due at the Tasty in just a few hours from now, after all, and I wanted it to be there.